**Rachel Dove** is a tutor and romance/rom-com author from West Yorkshire in the UK. She lives with her husband and two sons, and dreams of a life where housework is done by fairies and she can have as many pets as she wants. When she is not writing or reading she can be found dreaming of her next research trip away with the family.

## Also by Rachel Dove

*Fighting for the Trauma Doc's Heart*
*The Paramedic's Secret Son*
*Falling for the Village Vet*

Discover more at millsandboon.co.uk.

# SINGLE MUM'S MISTLETOE KISS

RACHEL DOVE

MILLS & BOON

First published in Great Britain 2022
by Mills & Boon, an imprint of HarperCollins*Publishers* Ltd,
1 London Bridge Street, London, SE1 9GF

www.harpercollins.co.uk

HarperCollins*Publishers*
Macken House, 39/40 Mayor Street Upper,
Dublin 1, D01 C9W8, Ireland

Large Print edition 2023



Special thanks and acknowledgement are given to Rachel Dove for her contribution to the Carey Cove Midwives miniseries.

ISBN: 978-0-263-29717-1

05/23

MIX
Paper | Supporting responsible forestry
FSC™ C007454

This book is produced from independently certified FSC™ paper to ensure responsible forest management.
For more information visit www.harpercollins.co.uk/green.

Printed and Bound in the UK using 100% Renewable Electricity at CPI Group (UK) Ltd, Croydon, CR0 4YY

In memory of Jean Wrigglesworth,
who loved life, and reading
Mills & Boon. Dearly missed
and for ever loved by all.

Also for Oliver, my darling dog
and writing buddy. Run free on the
rainbow bridge, my little love.
Max will look after you.

# CHAPTER ONE

*Lord, these chairs* are *surprisingly uncomfortable. I'll have to mention it to Nya when I'm back at work. Get the cushions restuffed or something.*

Marnie adjusted herself in the seat, smiling at the other visitors in the waiting room as she waited for her turn. It was weird to see the other side of the curtain, so to speak. It was health visitor day, and she was here as a patient. A new experience for her. She felt a little weird, used to being the one helping new mums.

It was a cold December day, one that she'd been looking forward to since having her baby. The last time she was here, she was giving birth. Her baby being delivered by the colleagues she loved and cherished in her own place of work. She loved the symmetry of it all. It gave her a real sense of belonging, and her previously wanderlust-filled heart was not only healing, but it was also full. She'd gone from broken-hearted single midwife, to becoming a mother in the community that she loved and lived in.

She'd come so far from that beach in Bali. From the girl laughing in the photos with Oliver, as the world's sights and landmarks provided the backdrop to their trip snaps. Living with a lie she didn't discover till it was painfully late. She'd returned home with sand in her suitcase and devastation in her heart. Carey Cove had been somewhere to retreat to. Somewhere to start a new life, one she'd never thought would be on the cards.

Now she was the rather tired hormonal mother, sitting with the other new mums and babies in the beautifully festive decorated waiting room, waiting for her six-week check with the other patients. Her back was aching, and the seat of the thinly cushioned chair was too rigid for her still recovering body. Violet snuffled in her arms, and she adjusted her to stop the arm cradling her going dead. Her newborn daughter settled straight back to sleep again, and, looking at her, Marnie was overwhelmed by a rush of love once more.

She often felt it. It slapped her right in the face sometimes. When she looked at her child and wondered how on earth she'd got so lucky. PCOS had been part of her working and professional life for years. She'd held many women, crying over their condition. What it meant for their fertility. For the children they wanted but couldn't have. She was one woman who didn't take her fertility for granted, ever. She'd been lucky, she knew. So lucky, and whenever she looked at Violet, she was reminded of that.

Yesterday she'd cried tears of pure joy because Violet had sneezed in a cute way. The day before that, it was seeing her tiny little outfits all freshly washed and drying on the radiator. She was besotted with her, utterly in love with the wondrous bundle in her arms. She still couldn't quite believe she was a mother. She'd always thought that it was something that would never happen to her, so every sneeze, every little snuffle—it was all just so joyful.

She'd given birth here, of course, so she had gone through every experience she could here. In the best place too. Her place. Hers and that of the women who ran the place. The men too, of course, but everyone knew who the real bosses were. Even St Isolde's, the hospital in Falmouth they worked with, knew how instrumental Carey House was in the care of the patients in the community and beyond. Theo was one of the main doctors there, and she knew that Carey House held a special place for him too. Everyone felt it, the minute that they walked through the doors.

She wondered how her replacement was getting on. She hadn't spotted any new midwives there so far, and the girls had been very quiet on the work front. They kept telling her to forget the place, and her patients. That all was in hand, and she should just enjoy the time with her child. Which she was doing, but she couldn't quite quell the curiosity about her replacement. They were in their second week now, she knew they'd be feeling pretty settled already. Carey House didn't have the need for many agency staff; once people came, they tended to stay. It spoke a lot for the place, she thought. Whoever was taking over her role, she knew that they'd enjoy their time there. It was hard not to.

Even now, the waiting room felt more like a cosy sitting room rather than the usual colder, clinical waiting areas health buildings usually defaulted to. Here, it was more like coming to a boutique hotel to have a baby. It was a unique place, and the staff who ran it worked tirelessly to keep it that way. It wasn't uncomfortable sitting here waiting, aside from the slightly lumpy chairs. She found she was enjoying being an observer for once. Violet was great, but with her cottage being the only occupied house on her lane, it was quiet. Violet couldn't exactly talk back yet. It was nice to be amongst the chatter of life once again.

The other mums were chatting amongst themselves. She heard the odd snatch of conversation. The whole place was festooned in Christmas decorations, which reminded her that she was normally trimmed up at home by now. She'd made a start, but, with Violet to care for, she was finding it a little harder to get her bigger jobs done. She had enough to do sanitising every surface in the house when she got a little restless or bored. Not that Violet was an annoyance. She couldn't stop looking at her daughter, marvelling at every little noise and facial expression.

Babies were far from boring, but she was missing the routine. The laughs with her colleagues.

The twinkly lights from the tree nearby were making her feel cosy, and tired. Hopefully she'd be able to get a nap in that afternoon, while Violet slept. She could leave the rest of the decorations to another day. She'd made a start with adorning her fence with cane decorations, but some of her other pieces took a bit of putting together. It wasn't as if she had neighbours to compete with. It was just her and Violet on their little lane. She had no one to impress but her babe, and that was just the way she liked it. One of the women laughed across the room, and she found herself listening into their conversations.

'A whole six hours! Wow, I wish mine would sleep that well. I swear, I slept in front of the dryer the other night. The sound was the only thing keeping this little monkey from screaming the place down!'

'Don't talk to me about cracked nipples. With my second, I was about ready to punch the next person who called me Dolly Parton. I was in so much pain. What's the point of huge jugs when they feel like two hard rocks? I swear, I don't know how we conceived our third after that. I was done!'

A giggle of laughter rang out now and again. Women swopping horror stories. Marnie sat there, cradling Violet to her, enjoying every minute. Now she wasn't just a bystander to these stories. She didn't have to just nod and empathise any more! Now she had her own stories to share. Although she was feeling pretty smug at the moment. Things were good. Hardly any hormone swings at all. If she could get some decent sleep, life would be pretty perfect. Just as she'd hoped it would be, after Oliver, her no-good lying ex, after everything she went through to become a mother. She felt as if Violet was the prize, her future dream realised by her and her alone.

'These chairs are a bit hard, aren't they?' Another mother sitting next to her shuffled in her own seat. Her baby was sitting at her feet in his infant carrier, wearing a little blue outfit of dungarees and a giraffe T-shirt. He was fast asleep.

'I'm glad you said that. I thought it was just my creaking back,' Marnie replied with a smile. 'I love his outfit.'

'Aw, thanks, it's his second change of clothes this morning, to be honest. We had a bit of an explosive-number-two incident this morning. I filled a washing machine load with everything he marked. It was up to his ears!'

The two women laughed together. 'I'm Vicky, by the way, and the poop machine is Benjamin.'

Marnie shook her hand, feeling the warmth from her fingers wrap around her own.

'Marnie, and this is my little Violet. Is he your first?' Marnie didn't recognise her, but she was on maternity leave from Carey House, the cottage hospital she was currently sitting in. She didn't deal with every mother who came through the doors. She felt a pang at missing work, but it soon passed when she looked at Violet again. She was in no rush to get back quite yet. Delivering babies was addictive, and it was nice to be back in the butter-coloured stone building that she loved, but she wasn't in that much of a rush for her maternity leave to be over. She wanted to enjoy every moment with her baby daughter before things got hectic. 'Violet's mine.'

'No, I've got a three-year-old too. Jaxen. They say you forget how tiring it is, your first. Feels like my firstborn sometimes, when he's screaming at three a.m. It's amazing what you forget. Or block out!' Vicky laughed again, and Marnie nodded.

'Ah, well, it's all new to me still.' She

didn't let on that she worked there as a midwife, had delivered hundreds of babies inside these very walls. 'It might just be the hormones, but I'm loving every minute.' Marnie knew it wasn't just the hormones, but she wasn't about to wax lyrical in the waiting room. Even at three a.m., when she was feeding her daughter and feeling as though she hadn't slept in a month, she knew it was worth it. Every little bit of her journey had given her the perfect little bundle in her arms, and she didn't take a second of it for granted. Or forget how long she'd longed for her. How much effort it had taken to get there on her journey to motherhood.

'Nothing like it, is there?' Vicky agreed, looking down at her son Benjamin who was awake now and busy trying to eat his little fist. 'I swear, I never thought I'd have another. You know, you get busy, money gets tight. He's worth it though.'

'I totally agree,' Marnie said, thinking about the months of IVF she'd gone through. She'd go through it again tomorrow to get to be sitting in this chair today. 'It's the best. Tiredness and poo incidents aside, of course.'

The two women got to chatting, and Marnie found that she was really enjoying herself. It was like being admitted to a club that she'd been denied access to before. She felt as if she'd been looking through the windows of parenting as a bystander for so long. Wondering whether she would ever get her chance, like millions of other women out there who found it so easy. Sometimes she couldn't believe she'd done it. She had arrived, and her baby had been delivered by her colleagues in this very place. Well, had she taken a longer walk, Violet might have been born on the beautiful front lawn! It had felt so right, as if she'd come full circle.

She was a member now, a fully-fledged mum. No longer would she have to listen to anecdotes of sleepless nights and other parenting nuggets that she wasn't a party to. She finally had the status that she'd longed for and feared she'd never have. Mother. Vicky was telling her about the local nursery in the area that her son went to, but she suddenly fell silent.

'Vicky?' she asked, wondering why she was staring across the room doing a pretty good impression of a goldfish out of water. 'Are you okay?' Benjamin passed wind and even that didn't rouse Marnie's waiting-room companion. Her lips moved, but nothing came out. Marnie looked around the waiting room. The mothers were all aflutter in the room, she noticed now. She felt as if the wintry temperature had risen by a few notches, felt the tension change in the air. At her side, Vicky's elbow jutted out, knocking Marnie's.

'What?' Another nudge, and Marnie turned to see what she was looking at agape. Another new mum patient had just come back into the waiting room, and a man was standing talking to her, his back to them. Marnie noticed his clothing and frowned. He was dressed in the staff uniform. 'Who is that?' she half mumbled. She took in his rear profile without meaning to. It was hard not to; the man was like a side of beef. He was easily six feet tall. She could tell from her sitting and gawking position. Trust her to be on maternity leave when they had a hot locum in.

A locum… *Oh, no.* Was this muscled Adonis her temporary replacement?

'Have you seen him before?' she asked Vicky from the side of her mouth.

Her replacement was supposed to be in situ already. Perhaps he wasn't hers. Or rather, her replacement. Marnie shook her head. Maybe the hormones had resurfaced a little bit. She was a teeny bit hot and bothered by the vision in front of her. She kept wondering what he looked like. The back of his head was pretty enough. Short dark brown hair atop a strong neck and a thick set of shoulders, leading down to a well-packed torso.

'No, and I don't know where they got him from,' Vicky breathed at the side of her. 'But they should get more like him. He's easy on the eye, isn't he?' She didn't whisper the last bit, and Marnie was sure that she saw the man's back stiffen. She could see the set in his shoulders rise somewhere around his earlobes. She blushed despite herself.

*Caught ogling a man on her six-week check. She could just imagine what her colleagues would make of that.*

She fanned her face with her free hand, trying to circulate the air back into her lungs. That was not what she was here for.

The mystery Adonis kept talking to the mother, giving her a pamphlet while the patient thanked him. Marnie focused back on Violet, trying to distance herself from the conversation. She never earwigged in waiting rooms, not on private conversations. She wasn't about to start now. Or here. She was here as a new mum, just like the others. Here for her six-week check, something she'd been looking forward to. Another club she was now a member of after waiting and wanting Violet so long. She was still on leave. It wasn't her concern, not yet.

*Who was he, though? Had he come from an agency?*

'See, you can't even speak. How come he works here? It's a bit of a waste, if you ask me. He should work in the fertility clinic.' Vicky was obviously not afraid to speak her mind. Or one to lower her voice. 'Cart *before* the horse, that way.'

*God love the Cornish candour,* Marnie thought to herself as she saw the man turn slightly in their direction. His ears were obviously burning. Quite obviously in fact. The tips of them were bright pink. She cleared her throat to stop the laughter that threatened to burble up as she looked away quickly. The man returned to seeing the woman and the baby she was holding out.

'I think he heard you.' She smiled at her rather funny seat-mate. 'I don't know who he is, I've never seen him before either.' She didn't bother divulging her bemusement and slight irritation about it either. Or the fact that she'd watched the way his shoulders had bunched the material of his uniform as he'd turned towards them. She found herself wishing she'd had the energy to put some make-up on that morning. She knew she didn't look her best. Sleep deprivation did that, despite all her planning.

*Wait, what? It's just a man, Marnie! What do you care anyway?*

'Well, I think you might be about to find out.' Vicky broke through her flip-flopping thoughts as the man turned and set his eyes in their direction. And his rather long legs. She was wondering to herself what shoe size he was when his feet stopped right in the middle of the room.

'Heads up, ladies!' Vicky stage-whispered as he approached. The ladies in the waiting room all collectively sat up, smoothing down errant locks and reaching for compacts from their changing bags. Marnie remained frozen in place. She wasn't about to preen for a man. Even a huge hunk in midwife's clothing. She couldn't have moved if she'd wanted to. He was looking straight at her, and she couldn't seem to break her gaze away. Hazel eyes demanded it, and she found that she couldn't look away from them.

*Was this her replacement? Oh, her workmates were in trouble now. A heads-up would have been nice, ladies!*

'Ladies, if I could just grab a second of your time.' He nodded to the health visitor who was busy weighing babies in the corner of the room. 'Sorry for the intrusion.'

She heard Vicky mutter something along the lines of 'you can grab what you like' beside her as she nodded, almost mute. The back of his head was unfortunately not his best feature, as she had previously pondered. The front of his head, well. Wow. The man was gorgeous, for want of a better word. Fit, for another. He was like a huge tree trunk standing in front of her. Momentarily an image of her as a squirrel popped into her head, but she shook it back out when he continued talking. She tried not to focus on the shade of hazel in his eyes. It reminded her of the trees in spring, the ones that grew around the place. The green and the brown flecks in his eyes making a colour all of their own. One she couldn't quite place.

'I'm Ash Ellerington, the new temporary midwife. You might have to bear with me a moment, ladies.' He raised his deep voice to address the room. 'It's my first day here at Carey Cove, but I'm a very quick study. I know my predecessor is already really missed, but I hope that I can help while I'm here.'

His smile was charming, and Marnie watched the women all fall under his spell. Further than they already had from mooning over his physique.

*Well, he certainly has a way with women.*

He turned back to her, bringing his smile with it. She looked away.

*I don't think so. You're not winning me over.*

'Replacing who?' she asked, already knowing the answer but still not wanting it to be true. He was late, anyway! First day today? What the heck? He was supposed to have started two weeks ago! She thought of her patients, of her colleagues sharing her workload while she looked after her new baby and got to grips with being a single mum. The thought irked her. Why wasn't he here two weeks ago? Why had they waited for him, and not just booked someone else? The man looked around the room, noticing the obvious interest in their conversation.

'One of the midwives, maternity leave,'

he replied vaguely. And rather dismissively, Marnie thought to herself. She'd already made the decision to dislike him, it seemed. Did he not even know who he was replacing? The girls must have told him her name. She felt the pang of work stress down her spine and hated him for making her feel like this on such a good day. 'If you'll excuse me, ladies, I had better get on.' He half bowed at them, which made Vicky swoon at the side of her. Marnie kept her body rigidly straight, watching him turn and walk away.

*He had better be doing a good job. First day indeed!*

She watched him talk easily with a couple of mothers at the other side of the room, and she busied herself with her turn, her name being called to go and have herself and her baby checked. Soon she was focused back on her appointment and Violet. The six-week check was important, and Violet was hitting all her milestones. She didn't see the man again, and her appointment was over before she thought about him when it was time to leave.

She'd bundled them both up against the cold, and she was not long out of the doors of Carcy House when she heard her colleague's voice from behind her.

'Marnie, glad I caught you! Have you got a minute?'

She turned to look at her friend Nya and was shocked to see Ash standing beside her. She felt her eyes narrow in his direction instinctively. As if she were observing a cuckoo in her nest.

'Hi, Nya! I would have said hi, but I know you guys are busy.' She looked Ash in the eye. 'First days tend to be busy.' Her dig went unnoticed by Nya, but she was satisfied to see Ash wince.

Nya had since closed the gap between them both and enveloped her in a huge hug. Violet protested from the car seat in Marnie's hands. Nya bent down to look closer at the little girl. 'Sorry, my little beauty! We just really miss your mummy here!' She reached out and smoothed her blankets a little against the cold before turning her hundred-watt smile back to Marnie. She sure was happy these days. Marnie was so happy for her friend, and Theo was such a great guy. It was easy to love the two of them together. 'I didn't want to keep you out in this December weather, but I did want you to meet Ash.'

Ash stepped forward then and grew about a foot. He seemed to stand straighter as he locked his eyes on hers again. She thought of her irritation that this man was taking over her job. Go figure. She was trying to live her life *without* a man, and now she had one covering for her career. Seeing her patients. Still, it was hardly his fault. He was here now, that was the main thing. She'd be back before she knew it, and he'd be gone. The last man in her life that she would ever need. She rather liked the sound of that. Another piece of the man-free plan to tick off.

Nya was still chattering away animatedly about the comings and goings; about the Christmas babies they were expecting to arrive. Ash cut through her voice and held out his hand.

'Hi, Marnie. I'm Ash, as you know.' He blushed. 'Nice to meet you. I hear I have a lot of midwife skills to match up to.' He raised a brow, and she smiled politely right back.

'Nice to meet you, Ash. I hope—'

Then she made a mistake. A rather big mistake that took her completely by surprise.

She shook his hand. Now, it could have been the fact that she was blindsided, seeing this man and realising he was filling her shoes. It could have been the fact that while she was loving being a new and proud single mum, she was also a woman. A hormonal one at that. She could have put it down to many things, but she knew what she felt. It was as though a bolt of lightning had shot through her body. The very second he closed his fingers around hers, it was as if they had welded to each other. She'd gone from feeling electrocuted by his touch, expecting them to be blown apart, to being a hundred per cent certain that they were stuck together for ever.

When she managed to remember where she was, she focused on his face. He looked as confused as she must look. His lips parted, and his tongue peeked out, moistening his dry mouth. She understood. Hers felt like the Sahara. She swallowed, realising that she'd stopped talking mid-sentence. Instead of replying like a competent professional woman, she openly gawked at him instead. Their hands were still stuck in the handshake between them. Marnie seemed to slightly recover first.

'Sorry, I was going to say welcome, and thank you. I know everyone will make you feel at home here—it's our thing,' she said in a rush, and that was when she managed to get her fingers to move. She broke the contact, and saw Nya shooting her an odd look.

*What was wrong with her?*

Loved-up Nya was so happy. She hoped Nya didn't get any ideas. She wasn't about to be subject to some maternity-leave cupid caper. He could cover her job, sure. That was as far as she was willing to go with another man ever again.

Ash didn't bear witness to the women's little exchange. He'd already tilted his head to look at Violet. Marnie watched him grin at her daughter, and then the little madam grinned right back.

*She smiled! At him! Have I taught you nothing, Padawan?*

She would have to be having words with her progeny.

'Smiling already, eh? Clever girl!'

He pulled a funny face at Violet, and Marnie watched as her daughter showed her cover man a gummy smile. A full, beaming grin of pure happiness to see him. It was as if ruddy Santa Claus himself had peeped his head in to say hello. It made Marnie's heart clench.

*Yeah, post-partum hormones and Christmas don't mix. I'm one Hallmark movie away from being a total festive softie. I've been waiting for her to smile, and she gives it up to him? I hope it was just wind.*

She knew better, but even the midwife in her was willing to go along with the self-told lie.

*You're smiling away at our enemy, little one.*

She had expected her daughter to have her back, but obviously she was a sucker for a handsome face. Not that he was handsome, per se. Well, he was, if you went for the whole tall, dark and handsome package. Which she didn't.

She wrapped her coat around her a little tighter as the wind picked up around them. The summers here in Carey Cove were amazing, and the winters beautiful, but cold. Ash gave her a look of concern, but she ignored him. She didn't need his help.

'I'd better get her in the car.' She held the car seat a little closer to her body. 'Nice to meet you. Nya, call me.'

'You too.' He took a step back from Violet and her. 'It was lovely to meet you both.' He nodded to Violet. 'I'll let you get warmed up.' Still feeling frazzled from the excitement of her morning, and freezing rapidly, she looked at Violet. She was still looking at Ash, bundled up. It looked as if Marnie wasn't the only Richards girl to try to size him up. Violet was staring at him so hard her eyes were almost crossed.

'Thanks.' She smiled at him while avoiding those hazel eyes and nodded to Nya. 'I'll see you soon, Ash.'

The two of them said their goodbyes, and Marnie headed off. When she was out of sight, she stopped and looked at the palm that had touched Ash. She could still feel a tingle on her skin that she knew was nothing to do with the Cornish winter.

She was still thinking about him when she got home. The jolt she'd felt when she'd shaken his hand was still affecting her now.

*What the heck was that?*

She'd had quite a crush on a few people when she was pregnant. Idris Elba in…well, anything, for example. She'd watched *The Avengers* on repeat. She understood that behaviour. She was a midwife, she knew all the stories, all the tales of weird cravings and urges. Crushes on celebrities while they were growing a human. But now? She was done with men. Ash felt like a fence post blocking her new man-free life. One where she delivered the next generation of babies and raised her daughter. All on her own. Just the two Richards women. They were going to be the Gilmore Girls, sans the cute and rather surly café owner. That was what Ash was. He was a café owner in the plot of her life. An unnecessary character that she knew belonged on the cutting-room floor.

*Lightning bolts? Pah.*

She didn't need it. Or want it. Plus, he was leaving anyway. He was a temp, filling in for her. She reminded herself of her earlier resolve. She was never going to be at the whim of a man, ever again. She'd had her baby without a man at her side. IVF had enabled her to finally follow her heart and fulfil her dream of becoming a mother. If she could do all of that single, then she wasn't about to change it.

Not that he was even interested, of course. She'd seen the odd look he'd given her after her handshake. Violet liked him, but she was a fickle baby. Her mother had plenty of time to teach her beloved child that a woman could do anything she wanted. With or without a smiling man with lightning-bolt handshakes. Ash would be gone soon, and she'd be back at work. Job done.

## CHAPTER TWO

'MARCH MADNESS,' I tell you. All these babies, it's the product of the March madness.'

Sophie fast-walked down the corridor, a delivery kit in her arms. 'Ash, you are in for a hell of a first day! Shout if you need anything!'

She rushed into one of the delivery rooms, the shouts of pain from the labouring woman inside escaping till the doors swished closed once more. Ash was left alone on the corridor. The six-week check clinic was done for the day, and he was now due to deliver his first Carey House baby.

'Good afternoon!' he said jovially as he entered the delivery suite. 'Mr and Mrs Evanshaw?'

The patient, a pretty young woman called Hayley, was sitting on the hospital bed, her legs flat in front of her. The monitor was strapped to her bump, monitoring the baby. Ash walked over to the printout, checking everything was fine with mum and baby. Mr Evanshaw was hovering by the far side of the bed, looking very worried. He was ashen-faced.

'Hi, Hayley, please. This is Tom.'

'Hi, Tom.' Ash held out his hand, and noticed how the expectant dad's hands shook. He'd already read her case notes. Mum was forty weeks plus five days, and more than ready to meet her first child with her new husband. Hayley was fine, relaxed even, but Ash could feel the tension coming off the father in waves. 'So, first baby today, eh, Dad?'

Tom grimaced rather than smiled back, and Ash patted him on the shoulder. 'Don't worry. I'm Ash Ellerington. I will be your midwife today. I'll be back to check on you both soon.'

He made the rest of his checks. Hayley was five centimetres dilated and progressing well. Baby was fine. A textbook pregnancy, it seemed. First babies were often late. He had a nice easy afternoon ahead of him.

He headed to the nurses' station. Nya was working on the computer. She stopped the second he approached and gave him a grin.

'Hi, Ash, how's it been? Your first patient going to plan?' She nodded her head towards the delivery suite he'd just exited.

'Smooth sailing so far. I just came to get my rota.'

Nya nodded in recognition. 'Oh, yes, I'll get one printed off for you.' She lowered her brows inquisitively. 'You didn't put down any days off you needed. Do you want to let me know?'

She was so nice, but wrong. She was assuming he had a life outside this place. He shook his head, plastering a jovial face over his features that belied how he felt.

'Er...no, I'm good. I don't have anywhere to be particularly.'

He didn't have a home either, really. The rental place he was staying at was nice, but one of a dozen places he'd stayed in over the last few months. He never stayed in one place for too long. It was how he liked it.

'At Christmas?' Nya sounded incredulous at the thought. 'Well, you won't be bored here.' She shot him a mischievous look. 'Things happen round here, especially in winter.'

Ash had no idea what she meant, but her smile brought out his own.

'Really?' Hayley's room buzzed, and his head instinctively turned towards the sound. 'Well, I'd better watch out for that.' He headed back to the room. Whatever magic this place held, he doubted any of it would rub off on his short stay. He was here to work and move on. Work, sleep, move, repeat. He had no time for magic. He knocked on the delivery-room door, and headed in. You would never tell by the smile on his face, his easy manner, that he was a man in pain. He liked it that way.

'Something's wrong,' Hayley moaned, her head slick with sweat. Tom was trying to mop her brow with a cold flannel. It just agitated her more in her discomfort.

'Tom, knock it off.' Ash was gowned and gloved, checking the baby's position. The baby's head was crowning, but Hayley was getting tired. The baby's stats were starting to change, and not for the better.

'Ash, what's wrong? Ash?' Tom was getting anxious, on top of his already jangled nerves. Ash needed to keep the situation calm, not scare Hayley. On top of that he had to soothe Tom, who was a neurotic mess. Things could escalate quickly in these delivery rooms. He thought back to the one he'd been in. How that had ended. It made him all the more determined to keep the parents calm and deliver their baby safely.

'Okay, Hayley,' he started, getting her attention while motioning for Tom to take her hand. 'Tom, I need you to stay calm. You're getting tired, and we need to get this baby out safely. The monitor is displaying signs of distress.'

'Distress?' Tom echoed, his voice a high squeak of panic. 'What do you mean? We don't even know what we're having, and now we have distress? Hayley, are you okay?'

Hayley had started to cry. Her contraction wasn't far behind her tears. Ash took charge of the situation.

'Tom, Hayley, look at me.' Both parents turned towards him, their fearful eyes wide. 'Hayley, on the next contraction, when you get the urge to push, I want you to push. If I say stop, I need you to stop. Okay?'

Hayley nodded, lifting her head up a

little as though she were preparing to go into battle. 'Okay.' She gripped Tom's hand tight. Tom was so pale he was transparent, his eyes bulging with terror.

'Tom,' Ash prompted, 'it's going to be fine. You're going to meet your baby any minute.'

That brought him back. He started to smile, nodding, and he reached for his wife's other hand. When the contraction took hold, Ash moved into action.

'Push, Hayley!' Tom said, his face streaked with tears now. 'Push, baby!'

Hayley's face went puce as she bore down, grunting with the pain. The head was coming. Ash helped her to deliver the rest of the little baby's face. 'Pant, Hayley!' he urged. 'Well done, I can see his head.' That wasn't all he could see. The reason for the slowing stats was wound around the baby's neck. Tom went to move closer to take a look. Ash saw his face as he took the umbilical cord in. He looked to Ash, and Ash shook his head at him. His expression telling him not to tell Hayley. 'Your baby is beautiful!' he said to Hayley, moving swiftly to pull the cord from around the baby.

'Is it—?' Tom began to ask.

'Perfect.' He cut him off with a smile. The cord was removed, and Ash could see on the monitor that the baby's stats were already climbing. 'On the next contraction, we're going to push some more. You tell me when you're ready, Hayley.'

Tom lost his squeamishness after that. He gripped Hayley's hand tight, one hand around her thigh as she pushed their baby into the world. Ash handed him to one of the nurses. He wanted the little one to be triple-checked. Put both his and the parents' minds at rest. It was a complication, it happened. He knew. But the baby was shouting, its annoyance clear at being removed from such a comfy home. It was fine. Healthy lungs. Glowing pink in colour. Shivering from the ordeal of being born, and opening eyes to see things for the first time.

Tiny fingers and ten toes. A little clump of hair on top of his head. He had a look of Tom, Ash thought. He held the little boy for a second, taking him in before putting him straight onto Hayley's chest. The little man let out a lusty cry, and when he locked eyes with his mother, he stopped. Decided to take to gazing at her instead. Tom had his arms around both of them, whispering barely coherent words of love and joy to the family he'd just helped create.

Ash administered the drugs to deliver her placenta. The nurses were cleaning up, Sophie brought in tea and toast for the mother. Ash worked methodically, completing the paperwork, and the checks. Making sure everything and everyone was taken care of.

He didn't try to listen to Tom, but he couldn't escape them. 'I love you both so much. Hayley, look at him. You did it.'

The baby let out another cry, and the pair of them broke into sobs of teary laughter. 'We're a family. Finally.'

Tom was cradling both of them to him, he and Hayley openly crying and smiling as they looked at their baby.

'Congratulations,' Ash told them both, looking at the bundle of soft blanketed perfection in their arms and feeling a pang in his heart that almost knocked him off his feet. 'You have a lovely little boy.'

'A boy!' Hayley beamed. 'Tom, you got your son!'

Ash could tell from the look on Tom's face that he didn't even care. He could have become the father of a bright yellow alien, and he'd have still had the same ridiculous, goofy expression on his face. Tom was just grateful that they were both here, and okay. That was why he held them so tight. They were his world. Tom kissed Hayley, crying again. 'I was so scared, Hayley. I felt helpless then.' He looked across at Ash, pulling himself together a little. 'Thank you, Ash, really.'

Ash waved him off. 'Hayley did the hard work. Congratulations again, the nurses will be in soon to check on you but if you need anything, just press the call button.'

He was just outside the door, collecting his thoughts before getting back to work, when Tom came out to find him. He held his hand out to Ash. Ash went to shake it, but Tom pulled him in for a hug.

'Thank you. I panicked, seeing that cord around his neck. You never even told her.'

He pulled back, and Ash gave his back a pat.

'No point in worrying her when she was already busy,' he said, deflecting the seriousness of the situation. Cords got wrapped around babies quite often, it wasn't as though he'd not seen it before. It was just weird that his first delivery had sparked so many memories of his own.

'She did really well. You have yourself a beautiful family there, Tom.'

It almost broke him to say it, but he meant the words that wounded him on the way out of his mouth. He always meant them. He cherished life. That was part of the problem, he guessed.

'Thanks,' Tom gushed. 'He's amazing. We're calling him Noel, after the season.'

Ash laughed. 'Perfect name for a Christmas baby. I like it.'

Tom nodded. 'Hayley picked Ashley, for his middle name.' Ash didn't know what to say. It hadn't happened before, in any of the places he'd delivered babies. A little boy in Carey Cove was going to have his name. 'I told her, what you did. We both really want to give him your name, if you're okay with it.'

Ash nodded, swallowing his emotion down before trusting his voice not to let him down like a hormonal teenage boy.

'Tom, I'd be honoured. Thank you.'

* * *

Later on, when they were coming off shift, Sophie pushed a photo under his nose.

'Here you go. Your first baby for the wall.'

It was a photo of Noel, dressed in a Christmas outfit with Christmas-pudding-themed mittens on his little hands.

'Wow, thanks.'

Sophie beamed at him. 'He's a little cracker, isn't he?' She passed him a pen, putting her bag over her shoulder and fastening her coat. 'Don't forget to put the details on the back. Night, Ash.'

'Night, thanks again,' he said, watching the other staff leave while the cleaners hoovered around them. A radio was playing somewhere in the background, Christmas songs playing on a loop of modern and classics. The Pogues started up as he unlidded the pen. He wrote the date, followed by the baby's name.

Noel Ashley Evanshaw
*7lb 14oz*
*Delivered by Ash Ellerington.*

He pushed back from the desk, getting up from the chair and pinning the photo to the board. A sea of babies looked back at him. He took in the faces of the families. All so different from each other. Siblings cradling their newborn siblings. Women giving birth with their mothers and partners supporting them, witnessing their family expanding first-hand.

Ash's eyes stopped on a photograph. Marnie. Her birth photo was up here too. He looked around, but no one was watching him. Taking the pin out, he looked at the photo closer. No man or mother in the room, by her side. On the photo, Marnie was grinning from her hospital bed, her colleagues around her bedside. He turned it over. Violet's date of birth was on there, just a few short weeks ago. Her birth weight, and her name. Under that, someone had written 'Marnie's miracle baby', surrounded by a love heart.

He didn't recognise the writing from any of the paperwork he'd seen before. He wondered whether Marnie had written it herself. He ran his finger along the elegant scrawl, and then carefully put the photo back in place on the board. It was near the photo of Noel and his parents. Ash moved the photo till it was a little closer to Marnie's. He didn't really know why. Maybe it was just that he felt as if he were working for her. Marnie would have delivered Noel, after all, had she not been on leave. Noel belonged to her too, he figured. That was why they were better together amongst the sea of happy faces.

It was coming to the end of his shift, and he was moving photos on a board. It truly was the weirdest first day he'd had in a while. That was without thinking about the thunderbolts he'd felt when he'd shaken her hand. A truly weird first day. Ash had loved it.

## CHAPTER THREE

ASH SIGNED HIS name with a flourish, a stack of paperwork to get through. He did a double take as he noticed the pen hadn't inked the page. Tutting, he threw the pen into the wastepaper bin at the side of the neat, colourful desk. He glanced back up at the photo collage on the wall, interspersed with thank you cards and little messages of gratitude.

Reaching across the neat and organised desk, he took a pen out of the pen pot and got back to work. He'd already started late, he didn't want to leave things unfinished on his first day. Carey Cove ran like a well-oiled machine, and he could tell the staff there were committed. He didn't want to show them anything less. As he filed the papers away, his eyes fell on the photo of Marnie again. Ash loved that she'd added her own birth photo to her wall, but he found it hard to look at just the same.

Babies were always the best part of Ash's job. He loved it. Bringing new life into the world, seeing people creating new families. Observing them adding to that family over time. Distracting nervous dads with talk of the sports results. Seeing the love and adoration, helping them to quell their fear and enjoy the moment when another person joined the population. Every new baby he delivered had him thinking of what his might be like, one day. How it would feel to be an expectant father in the room himself. Giving control over to the team of professionals, supporting his wife as they joined the parent ranks. He'd imagined it so many times. He couldn't wait. To be a dad, to be at the other end of the delivery room bed for once, waiting for *his* child.

He'd imagined everything.

Almost. He'd been stupid, he knew now. Gullible even. Naïve. He knew more than most expectant fathers. He'd seen it before first-hand. He knew the risks, the cruel twists of medical fate that could and did occur. It was life, and with that came death. It was part of the job. He'd known that. Or he'd thought he did.

Till the day he ended up leaving hospital, much later. A lifetime later. Alone. Then he knew he didn't have to imagine any more. The worst had already happened. His family hadn't started in that room. It had died. Despite his training and experience there had been nothing he could do to help. He couldn't save them. There would be no car seat, no slow drive home with their precious cargo in the back seat. He'd left tear-stained and broken.

His sisters had picked him up off the floor of his living room. Literally and metaphorically. They'd fed him, bathed him, nagged him to drink less coffee and more water. To remember to eat, to sleep. They'd cleaned his house, they'd cleaned him. Ash had barely noticed. He hadn't wanted to do any of those things for a long time. All he'd wanted was the family he'd created. The one that was gone for ever, before he'd even had a chance to enjoy it. He'd just wanted to be with them, in the early days. He'd missed them too much to function for himself.

When he finally had started to emerge from the cloud of grief, he'd known he'd had to leave. He'd had to change his scenery, to get away from the place that held so many memories of the life he'd loved but had lost for ever. His sisters had their own lives: families, friends, jobs. He loved them dearly, but he'd needed to move on. Somehow.

Babies always gave him joy, that never left him. He was grateful for that if nothing else. Grateful for the time they'd had together. He knew more than anyone how precious the moments were. So he'd gone back to his work, back into the delivery rooms filled with pain and joy and life. He'd put his own pain aside and gone back to fulfilling other families' dreams.

Ash pulled up to his new temporary home, turning off the engine with a deep sigh. He was bone tired, the quiet of the lane he now called home soothing. It was beautiful here in Carey Cove. From the moment he'd arrived he'd really liked the feel of the close-knit beauty spot. He'd felt the same when he'd walked through the doors of Carey House. It was a good place for him to be for now. A nice little place to retreat to for a while.

The staff seemed nice too, a welcoming, friendly bunch. Tight-knit without any cliques. Everyone who walked through the doors was treated with the same smile, respect and care. The midwives ran a tight ship, but his first day had been smooth. Given that he was two weeks late to the post, their reception had been both a relief and a revelation. He rather liked it there.

He'd gone through the day-to-day running of the house details with Nya, and he felt better about his second day. He had his shift rota, and now he was ready to settle into his new temporary home and looking forward to getting to know Carey Cove and its inhabitants.

Thinking about the people he'd encountered on his first day, he found Marnie popped back into his thoughts again. He looked down at his hand as he reached the front door, keys in his other hand. When they'd touched, he'd felt something intense. A zap in his fingertips running right up his arm. He'd just stood there in shock. Like a prize fish on a plaque. Glassy-eyed and open-mouthed. She'd looked at him in confusion.

*Probably wondering why I'd lost the power to control my face the second she took my hand.*

She was no doubt at home now, talking

to her husband about the total idiot who'd come to cover her mat leave. A woman like that would have someone to come home to.

He rubbed his tired eyes as he let himself into the cottage. The house he was staying in was so beautiful, even in the moonlight it looked inviting. Even though the windows of the place were all without light. He certainly wasn't expecting anyone to be at home waiting for him. The thought slammed him deep in his gut. Sometimes, in some places he worked in, it made it worse. Here, he felt oddly comforted by his new digs.

His cottage was at the end of a lane, with only one other house next to his. Perfect. The night was full of the sounds of the Cornish weather around him, but nothing else. No people. Not even a dog barking. It felt oddly welcoming. Calming. Less eerie feeling than the place he'd just left. He pushed the thought away.

It felt as if a whole lifetime had passed

since he'd turned up to his first shift that morning. As ever, he searched for the positives in his day, to push the dark, lonely thoughts away. Carey Cove was a definite plus point. The minute he'd arrived, he'd felt it. The magic of the place had soothed his tired bones. His first day at work had been great too.

*Marnie's hand. Wow. Where did that come from?*

The minute they'd touched, it had felt as if his soul had been lit up from the inside. For half a second, when he'd locked surprised eyes with hers, he'd thought he saw a flicker of something cross her features too. Her lips had parted, her mouth falling open before she'd pulled herself back tight together before him.

*Did I really see that?*

He felt sure that she must have felt it too. He remembered looking down at the floor to check for scorch marks. It felt as if lightning had struck right by their feet.

Madness, he knew. She was a colleague, for a start, he was the person covering her duties while she was tending to her new baby daughter. Violet, he remembered. She looked just like her mother. He'd seen it as soon as he'd set eyes on them. There was no way she would be single. She had to have a man at home, keeping the lights burning.

He turned to look at his neighbours' cottage. It was a carbon copy of his, but a better, finished version. He found himself drawn to the warm light spilling from the windows, the interior looking neat and homely. Christmas lights hung from the roof, twinkling and lighting up the neat painted wooden window frames. The house was well kept, and that extended to the garden. Oversized candy canes on red ribbons adorned the bushes at the side of the neat lawn, and there was a dusting of snow on the inside of the windows. It looked like a festive picture postcard, and made his pad look unlived-in and pretty unloved. Like he felt. At least it was pretty. Misery loved comfort, and he shrugged as he entered the front door, closing it behind him with a deep, tired sigh.

He switched on the lights, his half-closed eyes taking in his surroundings. The living room looked comfortable. On one wall there was a swept fireplace, an armchair placed perfectly in front. He could already see himself after a long shift of delivering babies, warming his feet by the fire. He looked around the hearth and saw that there was a wicker log basket containing two logs.

*Shopping trip tomorrow. Food supplies, wood. Get stocked up before the festive baby rush really gets going.*

He ignored his slightly empty stomach as he worked to get the fire started with the last of the logs.

Once the fire started to lick around the logs, he sat down in the armchair, his socked feet hanging over the end as he reclined back. He needed to get showered, drag himself to bed, but he found he couldn't muster the effort to walk up the stairs. He'd warm his feet first.

As always when he was settling into a new posting his thoughts invariably turned again to his lost family. His late wife, Chloe, their infant son, Sam. It had been several years since their passing, but the pain of their loss was lodged firmly in his heart. Less intense now, more of a dull ache, but always there, serving as a reminder to keep his heart guarded and giving him a reason to carry on with his nomadic lifestyle. And while he moved on, from place to place, he took comfort in knowing that, wherever they were, Chloe and Sam were together.

The fire crackled around him, the cosy feeling of the room amplifying as the warmth from the flames thawed out his overtired and rather cold feet. The silence of the room filled his ears, the occasional pop from the wood on the fire like a lullaby. He could just rest his eyes for a second…

*Bang! Bang! Bang! Bang!*

'Wha—?'

Ash's head snapped up from the back of his armchair. His neck cricked in protest as he wrestled his way out of the chair. The fire had burned down, the embers still glowing red hot in the darkness of the room.

*Bang! Bang!*

There it went again. He managed to put his feet onto the floor, tripping over the rug in the middle of the room he hadn't even noticed when he'd walked in. He got to the door just in time to stop the next bout of hard knocks.

'Hello?'

Ash saw the hat before he took in the officer's face.

'Good evening. Could you step outside

for a moment, please? We've had reports of a disturbance.'

'Disturbance?' Ash stepped out of the front door, past the police officer who had knocked him out of his slumber. 'Where? There are just the two houses, right?' When he looked across at the house he'd admired earlier, Ash was sure that he saw a twitch in one of the upstairs bedroom windows. A second later, he saw the light go off.

*What was going on?*

The officer was eyeing him, from his ruffled bedhead hair, his crumpled clothing, to his socked feet. 'We got a call that someone had entered the property here without permission. Are you staying here?'

Ash rubbed his hand through his hair, hopping from one foot to the other to ward off the bite of the cold weather.

'Er...yes, my first night—rental. I'm working at Carey House, as a locum midwife.'

The officer raised his brows. 'Carey House, you say?' Ash saw his gaze flick across to the other house, before looking beyond Ash to the open cottage door. 'Okay, do you have identification?'

Marnie hid behind the curtain when the man standing with the officer looked up at her window. Lunging for the switch for her bedside light, she flicked it off and hid.

*So there was someone there. How scary.*

She'd been up feeding Violet when she'd seen lights on next door. The knowledge it was supposed to be empty had had her reaching for her phone. Violet had fallen asleep in her arms and was safely snuggled in her cot. She went to peep out of the window again and she saw the mystery man handing over some pieces of white paper to the officer, who shone a torch on the documents, nodding his head.

*George! What are you doing?*

Surely Carey Cove's favourite officer wasn't about to leave the man there. George said something to the man, shuffling one foot awkwardly, before handing the papers back and holding out his other hand. The man stepped forward, away from the cottage, and the torch shone onto his features.

*Oh, Lord, no.*

Marnie squeaked loudly, embarrassment and realisation making her body jolt. Violet let out a solitary cry of shock and then fell back to sleep. The two men shook hands, and George turned away to his police car. She'd have to apologise to him later for wasting his time and dragging him out in the night for nothing. She held her breath as she watched Ash shake his head in bewilderment, turn and walk back into the cottage, and close the door.

He'd looked ruffled in more ways than one. As if he'd just been woken up. She blushed at the thought of her mistaken actions. The midwife covering her job was now living next door, and she'd just called the police on him! She'd had no idea he'd be staying nearby. Seemingly alone too. No other lights had come on in the house, and no one else had come out of the door.

*Was he here alone? Would he be alone at Christmas, or would someone come to join him?*

She shook off the thought. It wasn't her business. People had their own ways to live their lives. She knew that more than most. She'd recovered from a break-up, and her dreams had disappeared in front of her eyes. She hadn't been able to see past Oliver and his betrayal for the longest time, but when she had decided her next move, she'd gone with it with her whole heart. She hadn't stopped to think what people might say. The closest people to her were who mattered, and they were all supportive. Just as they knew she'd not made the decision lightly. They believed in her, and now she was living that dream, and Ash *was* here to cover for her. She didn't want him to feel unwelcome. That was not her, or anyone at Carey House. She didn't want to leave a bad impression of herself. It was an honest mistake.

Violet stirred again, and Marnie knew she would be up again soon. She'd fallen back asleep before getting her fill. Marnie rolled her tired eyes and moved away from the window to throw some clothes on. Once she was dressed, she went to scoop up her daughter. One sleep-mitten-clad hand was covering her face, making her look so cute Marnie had to remind herself that this little bundle was here, and hers. She smiled and lifted her daughter into her arms.

Heading to the kitchen, she reached for the baby carrier from one of the cupboards and popped Violet into it, pulling her coat over her to wrap them both up against the cold. It was a good job she'd been to the village bakery that day. She reached for the box of handmade mince pies from the polished countertop, tucking them into the nook of her arm before heading out to make things right. Hopefully she could get some sleep then.

Since Violet was born, sleep had been in short supply. Even a nap felt like a spa weekend. The last thing she wanted was to have an upset neighbour. She remembered the way her hand had felt in his, marvelling at the feeling of familiarity and excitement it produced every time in her gut. She flicked a lock of blonde hair away from her eyes and knocked softly on the door. She didn't want to run the risk of waking him up again.

Ash's smile was the second thing she saw when he opened the door. The first was how good he looked. Unkempt, tired, but naturally handsome. It made her stomach flip, and her lips break out into a smile that matched his.

'Hi,' he said softly. He looked down at the baby carrier with a frown. 'Everything okay?'

'No, actually. I came to warn you about a crazy neighbour who calls the police on innocent people.'

His laugh was unfiltered, and amazing to hear. She laughed with him, her cheeks blushing with her embarrassment. And his friendly reaction.

'Ah, thanks. I'll keep an eye out for her.'

'I came to apologise properly; I had no idea that Mrs Quentin had rented the cottage out.' She looked down at the box in her hands. 'I thought you were a burglar.'

'Only on the weekends.' He smiled. 'You have no need to be sorry. It was an honest mix-up.' He frowned as he saw her shiver. 'You needn't have come out into the cold, especially with the little one.'

'I didn't want to leave…it. I wouldn't have slept.'

Ash surveyed her face, his brows knitted together pensively.

'Well, thank you. Please, come in?' She hesitated a second, the box still in one hand. He narrowed his eyes. 'It's really cold out.'

She stepped inside the door, Ash moving aside and closing it behind them.

'I'm sorry,' he said ruefully. 'I haven't had a chance to get any wood for the fire yet. Come through.'

Marnie followed him through to the sitting room. The fire was burning low in the grate, but the room was warm and neat. The recliner of the armchair was down.

*Was he sleeping in the chair when George arrived?*

She felt her cheeks redden.

'Sit down, please. Would you like a hot drink?' His face paled, but she was too focused on the offer of caffeine to notice.

'Oh, no, thanks. I can't stay. I just wanted to make amends. Here.'

She offered him the box of mince pies as he offered her a seat with a flick of his wrist. They both laughed. He took the box, his fingers touching hers for a split second. *Bang!* There it was again. The jolt. Ash licked his suddenly dry-looking lips and motioned behind her to the sofa.

He pushed the armchair back into its sitting position but didn't sit till she was installed on the sofa with Violet in her carrier. He opened the bakery box, and she saw his eyes light up.

'The best mince pies bar none.' She grinned. 'The bakery round here is amazing.'

He lifted one to his lips and made short work of it. 'Mmm… Wow.' He swallowed the rest of the tasty morsel, reaching for another after a pause. 'Thank you for these. You really didn't have to, though. I'm sorry if I scared you.'

'I was up feeding Violet anyway.' She rebuffed his apologies. He was being so nice about it all. He must have had a long day too, given his current look. 'I don't sleep much these days, thanks to little madam here.' She noticed he had lifted a third mince pie to his mouth, and she realised he was starving. 'Listen, the local bakery delivers.'

His eyes met hers, and she was once more looking at the hazel hue of his irises.

'It's really handy when you're on shift. The supermarket delivers up here too. I don't mind taking in any parcels you get. I'm around most days at the minute.'

'That's really kind of you.'

'I'm like that with every burglar I meet,' she quipped, making them both giggle. 'It's no trouble, honestly. It gets pretty busy at Carey House.'

'I got that idea. I like it there though; I get a good feeling about the place. Nya's lovely.'

Marnie's white teeth flashed. 'Yeah, she's the best. She's a good friend.' She patted Violet's back softly in the carrier. 'She supported me when Violet was born too, so we have a bit of a bond.'

'That must have been lovely to share.'

'Yes, it was all a bit of a rush. I'd imagined going into labour a lot, what with our experience, but yeah. I was definitely taken by surprise.' She noticed Ash was looking at her intently. 'She was safe though. That's all I wanted.' She saw his shoulders relax visibly. He was a heart-on-a-sleeve guy, she realised. It was nice. He'd fit in well with the others. She felt proud that he was covering her role in that moment. He was definitely an improvement on the neighbour front. Not that the stakes were high, given that she'd thought he was some light-fingered shadow in the Cornish night.

'Must have been a worry for you all.'

'Well, yeah, but Nya and the team had my back.'

'Does your partner work in medicine?'

It was a lame question, but she kept saying I. No mention of a 'we'. He was curious about the answer.

'No.' She shook her head. 'It's just me and Vi.' Her green eyes flashed with something when she spoke. Ash lowered his eyes.

'I'm sorry to hear that.'

Marnie's smile widened. 'Don't be. I chose to have Violet on my own.' When Ash's brows furrowed in question, she waited for him to quiz her on where the father of her baby was. He didn't. What he said next shocked her.

'Well.' He was smiling now, the last mince pie sitting in the open box. He offered it to her, but she declined with a shake of her head. He looked as if he needed a good meal. She hoped he'd take her up on the offer of taking his deliveries in. It would be quite nice to have someone in the house next door. Tonight had rattled her a little. It felt different now she had Violet to care for too. She felt a little more vulnerable. 'I think that's amazing. How's it been going?'

He sat back in his seat, as if he was getting more comfortable to hear her story.

*Wow, he really cares. He's such a nice guy. Oh, enough, Marnie. Surely it'll take more than a pair of eyes and a gor-*

*geous smile to make you even contemplate going near another man.*

She focused on the question, willing her cheeks not to burn. He was still looking at her, intent on her features. It made her oddly nervous. She wasn't used to the feeling. It wasn't entirely unwelcome, but what did it matter anyway? She might as well just enjoy the chat with an attractive man. Attractive with a capital A.

'Good.' He lowered his brow, and she caved immediately. 'She's amazing. I love being a mum. It's mostly great, but it is tiring.'

His face dropped. 'I'm keeping you up too.'

Marnie waved him away, getting to her feet. 'No, it's fine. I spoiled your evening. Don't forget about the deliveries, okay?'

'Yeah, thanks. If you're sure.'

Marnie walked towards the front door, Ash close behind.

'Of course, that's what neighbours are for.' She turned towards him as he leaned in to open the door for her, and she felt it again. That jolt. There was no mistaking it this time, or his sharp intake of breath. The one that matched hers. Her head had snapped around to face his, and his hazel eyes, so entrancing. As soon as she looked at him, she knew he'd felt it too. She'd known it the first time but had talked herself out of that way of thinking pretty quickly.

'Sorry,' he breathed.

'It's okay.' She was flustered. 'These hallways are pretty snug.' They both laughed, and the moment of tension fizzled away. 'Night, Ash.' She slipped out into the night, and he walked out to watch her get back home safely.

'Hey, I like your decorations.'

Marnie rolled her eyes. 'I made a start, but I normally do a lot more. I love Christmas, and it's Violet's first one. I still need to make the Cornish tree.'

'Oh, yeah? That sounds nice.'

She smiled at him. It was there again. That full, toothy smile of happiness she had.

She waggled her fingers at him when her key was in the lock, and she was gone. He found himself still staring till the upstairs bedroom light came on.

Sitting back on the couch, he looked at the empty box and thought about the night's events. He'd gone from being a suspected burglar to a neighbour she wanted to help. She'd fed him. He hadn't even thought about how hungry he was. And sitting with Marnie had been nice. She'd looked tired—maybe he could be a bit of a neighbour to her too. Being a new mum wasn't easy, he knew that much. Her being a mother on her own, in this isolated lane, he felt an odd surge of protectiveness towards the pair. There was no mention of a father, and she'd actively told him there wasn't one. People went it alone all the time. Working in medicine over the years, in his various roles, he knew how complex and unique family set-ups could be, and how they worked. Marnie seemed so happy; it was nice to see.

Ash couldn't quite believe that a man would walk away from her—was there even a man *on* the scene at all? Had there ever been? Oh, Lord, he was driving himself mad with his theories and wonderings. What was the point? He wasn't up for a relationship. Heck, he wouldn't even be here. He was here to cover her maternity leave, and then he'd be packing up and off to his next job placement. It was how he liked it, wasn't it? It made sense to keep moving. Keep things fresh, turn things around and move on to the next place.

He loved delivering babies, it gave him joy. A sense of satisfaction. Maybe even chasing a few little demons away along the way. Marnie wasn't the one for him, it was just a passing attraction. Sure, it had happened more than once. The jolt he'd felt both times was hard to ignore, but his heart wasn't in danger. He kept that firmly locked away. He couldn't even think about getting into a relationship.

Besides, Marnie was independent. He could see the strength and warmth emanating from her whenever he was around her. Felt it whenever his new colleagues mentioned her at Carey House. He'd been there one day, and he knew that she was dearly loved and missed. It made him all the more curious about what it was that drew him to her, and all the more determined to ignore it. It was just another job.

Picking up the empty box, he tidied up. Hopefully he'd get some sleep in his strange new bed. He had a busy day at work tomorrow.

As he got into bed later that night, turning off the bedside lamp, he lay in the darkness. Marnie's light was still on. He thought of her, looking after Violet, her blonde hair half over her face as she bent to kiss her daughter. He fell asleep, the light from the house next door the only light in the darkness around him.

# CHAPTER FOUR

'RIGHT,' MARNIE SAID, pulling off her rubber gloves and laying them over the sink tap. 'I think we're done, little madam.'

She looked down at Violet, who was half asleep in her snug baby carrier on Marnie's chest. They'd had a busy morning and Marnie was excited to get into the festive spirit. She'd slept like a log after going round to see Ash, and Violet had even slept in a little. The wintry weather was the perfect backdrop to her mood. This was the first Christmas she was going to have as a mother, and Violet's first Christmas ever. She was really excited to get organised and embrace the season. She loved her cottage, especially at Christmas when the whole place looked magical. Oliver had never embraced the season as she always had, so this Christmas was going to be different in many ways. All of them good, in her eyes.

As she passed the dining-room table, her fingers reached out to touch the silk of her mask. This weekend was Carey Cove's Guise Festival, and her mother had already offered to babysit Violet so that she could have a night off. She couldn't wait to have a night off. Feel like a woman first for the first time since she'd got pregnant with Violet. She was really looking forward to it and it was a great practice run for Christmas Eve. Sophie and Roman's engagement party was going to be huge; the whole village was invited, and everyone was full of support for the loved-up pair. Eager to celebrate it together.

She'd been on a cleaning and organising frenzy all morning. The 'lie-in' had made her feel like a new woman, and she was taking advantage of the adrenalin burst.

Once Violet was down for an afternoon nap, she adjusted the hairclip holding her short blonde hair back off her face and headed downstairs. The sun was fading, the approaching dusk painting the sky with stars that twinkled above her home. She loved the summer and the late sunsets, but in Carey Cove the season never impacted on her mood. Christmas was Christmas. It was always a good place to celebrate it. The people here made it so special.

She headed outside to the workbench she kept at the front of her house. She loved gardening and tending her home. It gave her peace. She gathered together the materials for her Cornish bush decorations. Violet would be happy for a while. Marnie smiled as she looked at her sleeping daughter on the baby monitor she'd brought out. She was such a good baby; she'd slotted right into Marnie's life.

She felt very blessed as she put the withy in the centre of the bench and got right to work. This was the life she'd envisaged. Last Christmas, when she was making these very decorations, she had been hopped up on hormones and scared to death at the prospect of the IVF not taking. She only earned a nurse's wage, and IVF on the NHS was not routinely given in her circumstances. For a single woman like her, it had made it a little harder too, given that there was no father involved. It involved more ingredients to bake the pudding, so to speak. It meant a lot to her; she could still remember how she had longed to know the future. She did that sometimes, at a fixed point in her memory. Making the Cornish trees outside her home, wondering what the woman who would stand there a year on would tell her if they could meet. If last year's her were here now, she'd tell her everything would work out.

'Everything worked out,' she repeated aloud.

'Yeah, looks good from where I'm standing. Very festive.'

Ash was standing at his gate, looking tired but bright-eyed.

'Thanks. Good day?' Her work curiosity was piqued.

'Yeah, great. We had a Noel come into the world, and a Holly-Mae. Sophie thought it was hilarious.'

'Aww, that's cute.'

'Yeah, I think so. You had a good day? Had anybody arrested yet? The postman, perhaps?'

'No.' She levelled a steely gaze his way. 'I like our postman.'

'Ouch.' He laughed. She laughed along with him. 'Well, I need to get in. I'm starving.'

He touched his hand to the gate but looked back. 'You eaten?'

She was just adjusting a twig when her stomach rumbled. 'Well, I…no.' She looked around her at the piles of decorations. 'I guess I got a bit involved in my project. I don't do well watching TV. Or relaxing, really.'

'You like to be busy. I'm the same.'

Marnie watched him wrestle with something. She could feel the tension emanating from him.

*Is he nervous?*

'Fancy a takeaway?'

*Whatever it was, it's gone now. Why are you here, Ash?*

She wanted to hope for the best for him, that he would just leave, and she would move on. The annoying part was how much he intrigued her. She wanted to reach out and touch him almost, as if touching him again might crack the puzzle.

'I bet you know of some good places that deliver, neighbour.'

*Was that a little flirtation, Ash? I mean what are you doing? This woman almost had you arrested straight out of your sleep. You were late to cover her job too.*

But she didn't seem too mad about that now. He'd had a good reason, but he had felt bad about it. Reliable was something that he disliked being called these days, but it was true. He was usually the best at whatever he turned his passion to.

It had kept him going these past few months. Helped him get up every morning and put one foot in front of the other. He was alone, but he didn't have just himself to think about. He wasn't here to romance the woman he was covering for. He was here to do the job and move on to the next one. Check in on those who loved him, visit them when he could. Chase the bad feelings away with a move to the next town. The next set of faces he would forget the instant he got to the next shift. The next place had a new sea of faces to get to know professionally, new ways of working, and quirks, to learn.

As he quickly showered and changed, he thought about his neighbour. She was bristly. Good at her job, he knew that.

Her colleagues were singing her praises, but he knew that they spoke so well of her earnestly. They all loved Violet, but Ash got the sense that Marnie was keenly missed. As much as they welcomed him in with open arms. She was quite a person to work out.

'Idiot,' he said to himself. He half threw the shampoo bottle onto the rack. He'd washed his stupid hair three times while thinking about Marnie in the shower. He was losing his mind. Maybe that was why he got dressed so fast. He even squirted himself with a little cologne, still in his suitcase from his last place. Where it had stayed in the case. He frowned, realising he was overthinking yet again. Running a comb through his short brown locks, he checked himself over. He looked a little brighter than he'd thought he would. It was the prospect of food. The company wasn't bad either, of course, but he knew how to lie to himself well enough by now. He was nearly as good at it as he was at lying to everyone he met. It came naturally to him now, which was the thing that worried him the most.

Grabbing his wallet from the dresser, he slammed his front door a little too hard, and composed himself when he realised Marnie was still outside. She was standing there looking at him, a box of decorative bits in her hands.

'Everything okay?' she asked him easily.

'Yep.' He nodded, as easily as drawing the breath that filled his lungs whenever he looked at her. 'Everything's great.'

'So, like this?'

Ash held up his first attempt at decorating the withy bush, ribbon and decorative pieces all spaced out perfectly on his design. It was actually pretty good.

'You sure you've not done this before?' she asked as he jumped in the air.

'Holy— Argh!'

He'd received another scratch on his

arm from the sharp leaves they were working with. He'd drawn blood already but brushed it off when he saw her looking. She knew it hurt. The first time she'd made one she'd been cut to ribbons. He flinched again, and she saw his hand pull back. A giggle erupted from her, her breath misting the air around them. It was getting on for time, the sun long gone. She snipped another piece of holly into the shape she wanted, trying to keep a straight face when his head snapped in her direction.

'Oh, find it funny, do you? This holly is lethal. I stink of apple. I'll probably get some kind of plant-mutation disease, end up with branches for legs.'

Another titter erupted from her chest before she could stop herself, and he glared at her.

'I'm serious! This is a decoration? I could use this thing as a weapon.'

'Oh, really?' she asked, trying not to let the laughter take over her voice. 'How?'

'How what?'

'How would you use a Cornish bush as a weapon? It's a cute decoration, a tradition!'

'So is bullfighting, and you don't see me doing that either.' He assessed his creation again, as a blacksmith assessed the steel blade of the sword he had just finished forging. 'I'm pretty sure if you threw it at someone, or them into it, it would hurt. The holly sprigs alone are lethal.'

Violet was still to get restless. She was lying in her Moses basket, wrapped from the cold and positioned so Marnie could see what was happening on the baby monitor screen. Marnie peeped over at her, taking the opportunity to try to stop laughing at Ash.

'True,' she finally said when she could trust herself to hold a steady tone. She clipped the last piece of holly into her efforts. 'Well, I think I'm done too. Food will be here soon. I'd better feed and change madam here.'

'Want me to clean up here?'

Marnie's heart swelled. It was kind of nice to have a bit of help.

'You sure?'

'Yeah, but if you hear a woman screaming now and again—' he pointed to the offcuts of holly waiting to be picked up '—just ignore it.'

She was still laughing when she was in the house, changing Violet. She liked this side of Ash. He was caring, intelligent. Kind. Understanding. Given that she had tried to have him arrested and removed from his own home, that was something. Even in the friendly little haven that was Carey Cove. He'd just fitted in, she mused. As if he'd been one of them the whole time.

The fact that she couldn't forget hit her in the face again. All of this, this ridiculous inner turmoil over him while he was here solely to cover her job while she was on maternity. Thinking about it that way, she actually felt a little judgmental towards him for how nice he was to her. More confusion. She had been pretty prickly. Him being late for her job had added to her guilt about not being there at work, even though she knew her colleagues were not the ones stressing over it. They were all really happy for her, and they'd obviously held the fort down in her absence.

She had to admit, though, she'd thought she'd meet her mat-leave cover in different circumstances. She'd assumed it would be a woman, which had been presumptuous of her, looking back. Was she so sworn off men that she didn't see them any more? Unless they were a barcode number on a vial of sperm, she hadn't really cared a jot about men. She reminded herself that, whatever this was or wasn't with Ash, life wasn't due another change. She looked herself in the mirror again, Violet in her arms looking cute in her 'I love Santa' sleepsuit. One of the women at work had bought it for her.

'You are adorable, do you know that?' She dropped a kiss onto her daughter's smiling face. 'Come on, time for us to eat.'

Once Violet was changed and dressed ready for bed, Marnie wasted no time in heading back downstairs.

'It's nice to have company, isn't it?' she murmured into her daughter's ear. She got the bottle she'd been warming and took it through to the lounge. From the window she could see Ash tidying everything away. As though she'd called him, he turned and looked straight at her. She gasped a little. The jolt definitely didn't need a touch that time. He looked back, his face blank on first look, but then his expression warmed into a smile. His cheeks were bright pink from the cold December night. It had started to snow a little more, and soft flakes now broke up the black glossy surface of his hair in the darkness surrounding him. Even through the glass, he looked clear to her. Crystal-clear and absolutely gorgeous.

She smiled back, before turning her attention to Violet. Once she was drinking heartily from the bottle, her little hand stroking Marnie's arm, Marnie relaxed a little. Violet always did that, up and down. As if she loved to be in her arms. Looking at her, she grimaced.

'Well, that was those hormones I was telling you about.' She puffed an errant hair back into place, her face a picture of embarrassment. Violet kept drinking, staring back at her with those beautiful blue eyes. Listening, Marnie knew. To her mother, who was still swirling emotionally because of the birth and was now lusting through the window at her neighbour, who was tidying up their—her Christmas decorations, not laying pipe. She blushed again at the thought of that, and then he walked back inside.

She heard him shake his coat off, tap

and remove his boots. He came through to the lounge and seemed to pause in the doorway.

'Please, make yourself at home.'

*That was a bit much. You might as well ask him about the pipe laying.*

'I'm just feeding Violet.'

He came in and took a seat next to her on the sofa.

*Interesting.*

She looked at the armchair, and he followed her gaze.

'Sorry.' He went to get up. 'I'll sit over there.'

He stopped halfway in his ascent because she'd put her hand on his leg. She yanked it back, wrapping it under Violet as if to keep it safe.

'No, sorry. Please, sit down. I'm just not used to company.'

He looked conflicted for a second, as if he'd sat there without thinking about it beforehand. She hated that she'd taken that easiness away. Even if she'd had to brace herself to ignore the feel of his leg against hers.

He sat back down but kept a little distance between their bodies. She reached for the takeout menus she'd taken down from the fridge.

'Thanks.' He looked at Violet, smiled at them both, and turned his attention swiftly to the menus.

'So are we sharing, or doing our own thing?' she asked. She was willing her own empty belly not to give her away. Especially in this proximity. Her stomach, however, had other ideas. She'd had a busy, exhausting day, and she needed nothing more than to stuff her face. She was even willing to risk it in front of Ash. She recognised the fact he was hot, but she was off men, so food won. He might as well be a unicorn really. A nice unicorn, but something she would never have just the same. So food it was. She just wasn't sure that he was ready to see her rip into her food like a rabid hyena.

'Well, I don't know about you—' A gurgle broke the conversation. Both sets of eyes, well, even Violet's eyes, widened. 'Listen, that was my stomach. I didn't get to finish my lunch today—we had a bit of a rush on.' His cheeks reddened even more than when they were warmed by the fire close by. 'I apologise for that in advance, ladies, but I am going to order a lot.'

He waggled his eyebrows at her, making her laugh again. She noticed he seemed happier when she laughed. She was noticing far too many things about Ash Ellerington. Full-naming him again. As if he were some earl from those regency romances she loved to read. Well, she wasn't an eligible miss. This wasn't a book either. She pointed to the menus in his hands and jabbed a finger at The Imperial Palace. It was actually a restaurant, but they delivered too. The food was to die for. She never usually indulged. Tonight, though, she had company.

'Chicken and cashew nuts, prawn crackers, spring rolls, plum sauce, please.' She started to burp Violet, jerking her when she remembered something else. 'Prawn toast too!' She scrunched her nose up as Violet let out a resounding burp the second her hand patted the little one's tiny back. 'There you go.' Noticing that Ash was standing looking at her, open-mouthed, she shrugged. 'I'm hungry too.'

*Wow.*

Ash had seen some things when he was dating, before he'd met the woman he'd married. He'd dated nurses mostly, when he was training. Working in close proximity, the unsociable hours. It happened from time to time. He'd been on some horrible, awkward dates. Especially around food. Which made it all the more surprising that he was really enjoying himself. Marnie had relaxed the second Violet had settled, milk drunk, and she could eat. She'd eaten a full plate full of chicken and cashew nuts, and she had a prawn-cracker shard stuck to her trouser leg. Ash kept looking at it, eating his own food as he watched Marnie eat her fill. Now, this wasn't awkward. He felt comfortable here, with her. Violet got cuter every time he saw her. Which was from afar, of course. He wasn't one to get attached to babies.

*Not any more,* a weak little voice inside him said.

He silenced it with a spring roll.

'Good, eh?'

Marnie was sitting back against the couch cushions now, Violet still in the crook of one of her arms. Lazing, Ash would describe it as. Drunk on milk. His heart squeezed, and he focused back on his plate, and the conversation.

'It's the best I've had in a while.'

'Ah, well,' Marnie breathed. 'I bet you get to taste a lot of different stuff though, travelling.'

'I'm hardly backpacking around India. It's all in the UK.'

'Still, you get to come to places like this.'

'True.'

'You like it here, don't you? For you temporarily, I mean.'

Ash looked around the cottage, and then stopped himself. It made it look as if he were thinking about her home. Not that he wasn't. God, he was just stuffed from all the food. Tired too. It had been a busy day. It was late. He kept lying to himself over and over.

'That bad, eh?' She jostled his elbow with her free arm, putting the plate down and stretching her arm out.

'No!' he said, a little too loudly. 'No. Of course not. It's…great here.'

'Better in summer.' She smiled, getting a faraway look on her face. 'I can't wait to introduce Violet to the ocean.' She caught his eye. 'Still, Christmas isn't bad either.'

The air changed in the room, but Violet didn't feel it as they did. She started to cry, breaking the eye contact that felt charged between them.

'She's tired. I'll have to try to get her down.'

Ash smiled, not knowing whether to be disappointed or relieved by the intervention. Judging it by the thick slab suddenly lying across his chest seemed unreliable at the moment.

'She's got an excellent set of lungs on her.' He leaned in closer. 'She looks just like you.'

'You think?' Marnie turned to look at him, and her hair brushed his cheek. He half closed his eyes at the contact. 'I think she does, but I didn't like to just say it.'

'She's just like you.' He looked back at Violet, who was looking right back at him. It was as if she were sizing him up.

*I can't be your daddy, little one. I'm just passing through.*

'Beautiful.'

She was so close. So very close. His arm tingled with the effort of not bridging the gap between them. Could she feel this, really? She acted as if she wanted to push him away from her for ever and drag her to him and beg him to throw her up against the wall. All at the same time. To push against her with his body, while she claimed his.

Could that really be in her eyes? Was that what this was? Why did this have to happen? How could he attempt to walk away from this intact? Without action, too? God, the world was so cruel it twisted his guts. She felt to him like a light, pulling him to its warmth. Violet snuffled, and her head turned back to her daughter. She moved Violet to the other arm, giving the other one a little shake before turning back to him.

'Would you like to hold her, before I take her up? I won't be long. She's already asleep.'

Ash's mouth went dry. The room shrank to half its size before his eyes. He felt trapped for a moment.

*Too much. I thought these things had stopped.*

'Er… I don't think I should. You know, I've just come from shift.'

He thumbed at his top, belatedly remembering that he'd been home and showered. Marnie knew that too, but she didn't comment.

'What am I saying?' He slapped his palm against his forehead, before gathering some empty dishes with shaky hands. 'I got changed. Listen, I think I should get some sleep before I forget something else.'

She called after him, telling him it was okay, she would clean up, but her voice on the stairs went unanswered. When she came back down from putting Violet to bed, the living room was clean, and empty. He'd left a note on the counter.

*Thanks for a great night, neighbour.*
*Ash*

* * *

He closed Marnie's front door with a slow click. He waited till he was at the bottom of her garden before he paused to take in a big shuddery breath. He'd had to get out of there. He could never have explained himself. Especially not to Marnie. Just before that, he'd been wondering if he should kiss her. Wanting to kiss her. Needing to.

Sam. That was what had sent him running from there as if the whole place were on fire. Sam's cold little face. Not pink, and full of life like Violet's. She'd been snug in her mother's arms. The happiest little baby. Sleeping after a busy day. Not like Sam. He'd never even opened his eyes. Never looked on the world, on a single human face.

When Ash had looked at Violet, he'd seen Sam's face instead and he'd frozen. The thought of holding Violet, a wriggling baby, in his hands when they'd held tiny Sam for so little time. He'd frozen to the spot, and then run for the damn hills. Left Marnie a vague note that anyone could leave. It didn't serve as a good ending to such a good night.

He'd been fine around babies before. It was his job, for goodness' sake. Why this one rattled him was a mystery he didn't want to poke at too much. He knew Marnie was a mother. One all on her own and happy with the outcome. Violet was perfect, and Marnie was a great mother. All of that was attractive to him, but not exactly what he was looking for. He wasn't looking for anything. Peace perhaps.

Tonight was a reminder of why he kept moving on. Why he didn't form attachments any more. Because they caused pain. To others. Marnie's face when he'd dashed away like some thief in the night. She'd been so close, right there. Lips inches apart. God knew when he'd be that close again, and what he would be able to do and not to do if they ever were in that situation again. Would she slap him for setting his lips on hers, as he wanted to?

He took another shower, for no other reason than he felt dirty for his cowardly exit. By the time he slipped under the sheets, his mood was even worse. He loved Sam, so much. He'd held him for the shortest time, but he would love him for the longest. Till he stopped drawing breath himself. After that too, if he had anything to do with it. He loved his wife too. They were gone, though, and being here alone in a strange new place reminded him that he was still here.

He turned over for the ninth time, his naked form now only half under the covers. He felt strangled in them, confined. He wondered if the woman next door was sound asleep or thinking about his abrupt exit. Or him. As he was her. Squinting at the clock, he rubbed at his eyes, and went to get a tumbler of whiskey to help him on his way to slumberland.

# CHAPTER FIVE

'HI!'

'Hey, you! Aw, come here and give me a hug!'

The two women embraced on Marnie's front doorstep, with Marnie ushering the two visitors inside. She'd been cleaning up all morning, waiting for their visit and using her nervous energy up on chores and little jobs around her cottage. A tray of freshly decorated Christmas cookies sat on a plate in the sitting room. They were iced with different designs—she'd had a bit of a creative morning to channel her thoughts away from her neighbour.

'Come in, come in! It's so nice to see you both! I need all the gossip from work.' Violet was in her Moses basket, kicking her little feet out from time to time as she lay watching the three women enter the sitting room. 'How are you getting on, Lorna?'

Lorna stepped forward, giving her a broad smile and an outstretched hand. 'Ok I think, Marnie.' Marnie settled the pair of them in the lounge, bringing a tea tray through to go with the cookies. Nya picked up one decorated to look like Rudolph, taking a bite and closing her mouth in pleasure.

'Wow, you've been busy, Marnie. I thought you sounded chipper on the phone.' Marnie blushed, looking away to pour the tea. Perfect action to hide from her friend's scrutiny. 'Lorna's doing great as our trainee midwife!'

Marnie took her friend in for the first time. She was searching now for clues, while she hid her own about Ash. Something was weighing on her mind; Marnie could tell the second she'd looked her mate in the eye.

'Glad it's going well, Lorna. I know it

can be a bit full on,' Marnie said smoothly, taking in Nya's companion fully now too. She'd already heard good things on the grapevine. Their vetting procedures were pretty thorough—anyone given a job was always a good fit. They weren't cliquey, or a cult, as it sounded. They were just a group of passionate, caring people who sought out the same. She thought back to her travels with Oliver, half a world and a lifetime ago. Even now, when she was still recovering her body fully from childbirth, and surrounded by the winter weather, she wouldn't trade it. Not for now. One day, she'd take Violet with her to explore.

Nya nudged Lorna from her seat on the sofa, pointing to the plate of cookies. 'Lorna, I'm sorry we're so informal, but you know Marnie's one of us.' She finished the cookie and headed to the Moses basket. Violet looked up at her with her gorgeous bright eyes, and Marnie felt a swell of maternal pride.

'Well, little miss Violet, you have grown!' She turned to Marnie, beaming. 'She's got a little bit more gorgeous too.' Marnie laughed.

'Well, I'm biased, but of course I'm going to say yes, she did.'

'Are you okay for Lorna to do the checks on Violet here?'

'Of course.' Marnie grinned at Lorna, to put her at ease. Everyone had to train. No one was born knowing how to be a midwife, not with modern medicine ever evolving too. She remembered how nervous she'd felt inside on her first few months of training. It was daunting, the job they did. Definitely not a walk in the park. The highs of delivering a baby though—the only thing that had surpassed that was giving birth to Violet. 'We're a team, right?'

Lorna visibly relaxed. Once she was getting on with attending to Violet, Marnie took the opportunity to quiz Nya further.

'So, how's work been?'

Nya, sitting next to her on the sofa, gave her the side-eye.

'What?'

Nya laughed. 'Come on, Marnie, how's work? We're here to check on you two! Don't be worrying, we're coping.' Marnie felt a pat on her arm. 'We miss you, of course, but Ash is doing a good job.'

Marnie willed her cheeks not to explode into colour. 'Oh, really? Not too good, I hope.' Her too shrill laugh rang out into the room. 'So, what's he like, then?'

'Ash? He's nice. Really good with the patients, he's quite intense about procedures and equipment set-ups, but that's not a bad thing. Methodical, but fun with it.'

'Sounds perfect,' she replied without filtering her thoughts. Nya's eyes were on her again.

'You must know him better than us by now, though!' Nya threw back at her like a casual bomb. Marnie turned, making sure Lorna wasn't looking. She was busy with Violet, noting something down on the tablet they'd brought with them.

'Why would I?' There it was again, the high pitch of her voice coming to the fore with her nervous energy.

'Er, he lives next door? You must have seen him around.'

'Oh, yes, of course. I don't know him that well.' She got the urge to ask more, but she knew it would be obvious. They didn't gossip about people, especially not temporary workers. 'He seems nice. How's baby Hope coming along?'

She was changing the subject, but she did want to know. The little one had been left on the steps of Carey House. She couldn't imagine leaving Violet on the butter-coloured stone steps, in any circumstances, but she knew she could never judge. She was ready for Violet, in a good financial position. She had a steady job in a career she loved and friends and family around her if she ever felt alone or needed help. Hope's mother had taken her there to give her the best chance at life. Marnie knew that was all a mother ever wanted because she wanted that for Violet too.

Hope was being cared for by Nya and Theo, who had recently discovered that they were interested in more from their relationship than friendship and co-parenting. Marnie was thrilled for her friend and boss.

'She's doing well, hitting all her milestones so far.' It sounded a little technical, but Marnie understood. Perhaps she was trying to keep a professional distance. She got that. She'd done it herself for long enough. It was hard, seeing everyone else have babies. 'She's settled down really well. Theo and I love taking care of her.'

The three women chatted easily for a few more minutes while Nya and Lorna finished their cups of tea and ate a couple of Marnie's Christmas cookies. Finally it was time for them to leave for their next appointment. 'Are you looking forward to the ball?' Lorna asked her as they were leaving. 'I've been told it's quite the event around here.'

'I am actually. Looking forward to seeing you there, Lorna. Bye, Nya.'

'Bye, my lovely,' she said, enveloping her in a huge hug.

'Call me if you need anything, a sitter, anything.' Two babies wouldn't be a bother to Marnie. It would be nice to have company for Violet too. Socialisation could never start too early, especially when you had a whole cove of people around. It might just keep her busy too. She seemed to get into trouble when she was at a loose end. It wasn't itchy feet, but something like it.

She thought about it later that night, once Violet was asleep, and she'd run out of cleaning to do. She pulled an old photo album out from the bottom of her wardrobe. Paris. They'd taken the usual tourist photo in front of the Eiffel Tower, Oliver pulling a funny face at the last second before the photo took. She looked at the snap, at her laughing into the camera at his antics. She couldn't say it had all been bad. It hadn't been, till the end. They'd seen the world together. She kept flicking through the album till she found what she realised she'd been wanting to see. The engagement photo.

Oliver had handed his camera to another traveller, asking them to take a shot of them on the beach. It was a beautiful, hot day. Her face was sun-kissed, her hair blonder than when they'd started out. She wore her hair in surfer chick waves then, which she'd kept pinned up for work. Recently she'd opted for a sleek blonde bob. She now had a different life, and it was a different woman who was looking back on that photograph.

Oliver had dropped to one knee, and that was that. Their magical moment, now a snapshot in an album and a fading memory in her head. Two weeks before they'd been due to fly home, the bubble that was Oliver and Marnie had well and truly popped. Instead of flying home to a wedding, and their life together, she'd returned alone and changed.

Had she been naïve, back then? She thought so afterwards. Scrutinising every moment of their last few days together, to see if she could pinpoint the issue. At the time, she'd thought she'd never recover. She knew differently now, but did that mean that girl on the beach was gone?

Marnie put the album away and looked out of her side window at the house next door. There were no lights on save for one in the lounge. She wondered what Ash was doing. It was quite lonely on the lane. She pondered half a dozen reasons to send him a text, but then gave up and decided to go to bed instead. She didn't know what to say anyway. *I'm thinking about you? What are you up to?*

She snorted and turned to her side in bed.

'Don't be daft, Marnie. For God's sake, just stick to the plan.'

She pushed her phone into her top dresser drawer an hour later, a dozen more unsent texts to Ash on her screen.

## CHAPTER SIX

WHAT A WEIRD week this was shaping up to be. Even for Christmas. Even for this Christmas.

'Overthinking Annie' was here again. Was this what happened to all new mothers, or just ones who had got a little bit smitten with their neighbour? Well, annoyed at first. Then intrigued. Smitten was right after that, even though the lightning thing had been there the whole time. She had no point of reference for that aspect. She'd never encountered it before.

So here she was, her first big night out, and she was wondering where Ash was. What he was doing. Thinking even. Ugh. It was annoying. So she'd come full circle. Annoyed, intrigued, smitten, confused, and back to annoyed. The sheer rainbow of emotions that she felt when she thought of him gave her post-partum hormones a run for their money. In fact, they utterly surpassed them in every single intricate way. Thinking of a man again. Great.

She huffed out a frustrated sigh. She would be back at work soon, back in something like her old routine. A working single mother, and a happy one to boot. That was the plan. She felt as if she needed to keep reminding herself of that these days. Given her current swirling head, she wished she'd done what she'd almost done. Called to cancel her mother, put Violet to bed and eaten ice cream and chocolate in front of the TV. A thriller, with no romance involved. She could almost taste the chocolate, but she pushed herself to get back to the confident woman she'd once been. She was perfect, just as she was. She was just having a bit of a wobble. That was it. A bit of a flirtation with a passing stranger.

She thought of her movie last night but dismissed the idea. No, Ash wasn't a spy. This was why she needed to get out more, and why she was pushing herself to go. She had been so looking forward to attending the Guise Ball before this. She had a feeling tonight would be different from the usual events though. She felt excited, and she didn't trust it. She needed the plan to keep her sane.

'You are fine as you are,' she said aloud to herself, and felt her shoulders straighten in response. She said it to herself the whole way there, till the venue came into sight. Then, her mouth felt too dry to utter a word. 'You…' She swallowed hard. 'You are sticking to the plan.' She took another step, a more confident one this time than she felt. 'You are fine as you are.' She bit at her lip. 'Now stop talking to yourself and go and have some fun.'

The nerves kicked in the second Marnie's heels hit the grass of the village green. She felt odd. Naked without Violet and her changing bag. Alien in her own body without her child with her. They'd been together for so long, she felt lost. Careful not to ruin her sleek bob, she secured her mask and felt instantly better. Shielded. It was a little more glamorous than a bag full of baby wipes and rattles too.

She walked slowly across the grass, surveying the scene and taking everything in. She'd been so rushed lately, busy with work and Ash. His sudden departure the other night had really bothered her. But then, the mere fact that it had bothered her so much was so irksome that she'd been rattled by the whole thing. Why did she care anyway? He made her nervous. Wooden at times. It was embarrassing. She just couldn't resist being near him, but she wasn't going to tell anyone that. She wouldn't need to anyway. This secret had an expiration date attached to it.

He was covering for her for a finite

time, not for ever. He rented next door, as temporary nurses often did when the occasion arose. He'd be leaving, to go to the next job.

Then she'd be back to normal life, and he'd be off to help at the next place. It would be a shame though. It was quite nice having a neighbour. Especially one like this particular neighbour. She chose to focus on the night ahead. She wasn't on show like she felt in her head. She was incognito tonight, and here to have some fun.

She nodded to a few people as she passed, enjoying the curious glances from them. They didn't recognise her! The mask and her now no-longer-pregnant body were enough to make people take a second look. She quite liked it as she walked under the hundreds of twinkly lights, all adorned around the place. The Christmas tree was all lit up too, the perfect Cornish Christmas postcard scene. It was an amazing backdrop to the ball going on around her. Carey Cove was transformed for the evening, and the people with it.

She herself felt like a different person. Free, confident. Sexy. It wasn't all breast pads and bath books, she knew. She told her patients often enough. To remember the woman inside the mother. She was actually stupidly glad she'd made the effort tonight. Violet was safe and being adored by her smitten grandmother, Marnie was wearing a nice dress, and she was going to jolly well enjoy it.

Enjoy it she did too. People-watching at parties was one of her favourite things to do. When the room was a happy one, anyway. She gazed at the masked people for a while, trying to work out who was who. In the end her efforts were futile, so she started to watch their actions instead. People were bolder wearing a disguise, she decided. It was quite daring. Nothing risqué of course, but there were more than a few longing looks, she thought.

Maybe she was just feeling the post-partum effects again. She decided that she might have to keep using that line for a while. Especially given her recent day-dreams. She needed to shake off everything for a few hours. Stop watching life and get back into living it.

As if fate was conspiring with her for the evening, the next song to come on was one of her favourites. She didn't even try to stop her feet from heading to the dance floor. Normally she'd need a couple more drinks before she started making shapes, but the mask was a little protective shield. She felt great!

Marnie swayed along, lost in the music the minute her eyelids closed. God, she missed dancing. She used to love going out with the girls, letting their hair down and dancing the night away. It felt like so long ago now. Oliver had changed things. She'd lost pieces of herself, for nothing. She smiled as she moved to the beat, feeling oddly smug at the thought. She'd come through it, and now she was dancing again while her child slept. Safe and sound. What more did a woman need?

She opened her eyes as someone brushed their arm against hers, and her smile dimmed. She was dancing in a sea of couples. She hadn't noticed it before. She felt as though her joy had been cut off. A little fish, swimming alone. She tried to shrug the feeling off. She shouldn't have had that glass of champagne when she'd first arrived. She'd glugged it for her nerves, but now she'd had one thought of Oliver. Not even Oliver, she reminded herself. Hell, if he were on this dance floor she'd be sinking her heel into his stupid foot and walking away as fast as her legs could carry her. She didn't long for him. Not any more. She did get the sense that she was missing something though, and she was back to feeling…

Well, she didn't know what she was feeling, but she didn't get a chance to prod at it. As she turned to head off the dance floor, and was striding towards another drink, something stopped her. Well, someone. Masked, tall, dark. Male.

*Who was this guy?*

She thought she felt a spark of recognition, but the man kept coming before she could get a good enough look.

She didn't need another look. She knew half a second later exactly who the man behind the mask was. She would never admit it, but she knew that, right now, she could pick Ash Ellington out of a crowd of any other men in the world. The truth of that fact rattling around her brain scared her to her core. It was the one thing she didn't want. His hand closed around hers, pulling her gently towards him. She knew the second his skin touched hers. The man was Ash. It was as if he'd charged her up from the inside. She felt as if she were glowing brighter than any light on Earth or above. Zap. The power of Ash's hand in hers. It was unmistakable. Even when she didn't recognise him, she knew him above anyone else. This was so far off her plan she might as well tear the thing up.

'Dance with me?'

That was all he said. She didn't even answer. The moment her feet moved in his direction, his hand was taking her free hand in his and twirling her. His hands were soft, but she felt the power in his easy grip. The warmth of his hand on her hip as he steadied her on a spin, her laughing as he waggled his eyebrows at her above the mask.

The song changed, but their steps didn't falter. She tried to focus on the eyes behind the mask, the cut of his suit, as if that would give her a hint. A reason why this man made her feel so alive, what his deal was. Every time they saw each other, she needed more. To know more. To work him out, and how to stop his handshake from turning her into a bumbling idiot too. Not much to ask from a very confused and slightly overtired mother, surely?

She felt the thoughts float like feathers before she could catch them. His hands kept reaching for hers, twirling, dancing, and moving around each other. The other ball-goers were there, Marnie knew. She knew she was still on the village green; she could see the green brilliance of the Christmas tree reflected in the lights adorned around every tree and post. Reflected in every bauble and bright outfit of the guests. She knew where she was, that they weren't alone. They were not the only people there.

It felt that way though. Slowly, song after song, beat after beat. Every touch they shared; their bodies never not connected to the other. The mask helped her daring side come out to play, and Ash matched her step for step. They danced as though they had done it for ever. The night went from slower songs to bigger beats, their dancing getting more fun and playful as the night wore on.

Marnie was hot, parched and she had laughed till her sides hurt. Her masked companion had come in like a bolt from the blue, and it had made her night. Most of the night, she thought as she caught sight of her watch under the lights. The rest of the dance floor were still going, the energy of the whole place in full frivolity. Ash nodded his head to the side, pretending to mop his brow theatrically. His eyes were bright beneath the mask, and she could see his heaving chest matched hers. He'd enjoyed it just as much as she had.

'I might need a minute,' she admitted over the noise of the music. He laughed, a deep rich sound she wanted to replay the instant it was over. When he reached for her hand, she took it, laughing as he led her off the dance floor. He led them away from the noise of the party and into a quiet, moonlit corner. Shielded from the noise, thcy caught their breath, still laughing.

'I'm really glad I saw you,' he said, pulling her a little closer behind a tree as a loud trio of people heading home weaved across the grass nearby. 'I wanted to apologise for the other night. I didn't mean to rush off the way I did. I enjoyed myself, I wanted you to know that. I feel bad for how it ended. I guess I was afraid I might pass out and drool into the spring rolls.'

He looked away, even when she attempted to smile at him. She got the distinct impression there was a lot more to the story of Ash. She ignored the questions within her. When it came to him anyway. She had told herself that it was just because he was helping her out, with work, even at the house. Ash was a neighbour, a friend. The tags she'd assigned to him on the way to the *Don't go there* bin she kept for men and romantic entanglements these days. Her last interaction with a man had involved a test tube and she had sworn to herself she would not break that rule. Even though they had just danced like lightning bolts, fast and full of electricity.

'Oh, that's okay.' Marnie was having trouble concentrating on his words. The proximity of him was overpowering her senses, and her strict 'no man' rules. She was drinking him in, the closeness of him. How good it had felt to be in his arms, twirling on the dance floor together. It wasn't just his body though, or the way he made her feel.

How did he make her feel? As if she were plugged into a damn light socket, the electricity coursing through her skin wherever he touched her. It wasn't just that, or the feeling that he was feeling the same jolt, the same sparks. It was his eyes that held her attention too. Intense, lustful flashes even, and something else. He looked upset, pained. Was he feeling the same doubts? Did he have the same rule about not getting involved with a woman? He didn't stay in one place, after all. What would be the point?

She wanted to ask him everything, but she didn't want to hear the answers either. Nothing good could come of it. Still, the sensation that he was going through something was unmistakable in his expression. She didn't want to care, but she did. So much. She felt alive when she was with this man. She felt things she'd never felt with Oliver, and that knowledge was something even her stoically single brain couldn't deny. She wanted to comfort him, be the one who chased his cares away. Even if it was just for the night. It couldn't be more: they were worlds apart, and soon he would be miles away too. Possibly making some other woman's heart fill with longing.

*Ugh.* Her heart clenched at the thought. She had no claim on him, but the thought of him with another woman made her heart hurt.

Would they feel the jolt from his touch

too? She doubted it. She doubted that there were two other people on the face of the earth who felt like this in the other's presence. 'It's okay,' she repeated, her voice barely a whisper. He looked from her eyes to her lips, and back again. His tongue darted out to lick the dryness of his own full mouth, and she followed the movement as if she were starved. Her tongue tingled with jealousy. 'Ash…'

She wanted to smooth the crease from his brow, but her hands didn't move. 'Did something happen? Is that why you left?'

She thought of their lips, so close on that sofa. *So close.*

'Was it something I did?'

'No, of course it wasn't you,' he cut her off softly. Once more his beautiful hazel eyes focused on her mouth.

*Could he see the words hidden behind her lips, begging for release?*

'It was me.' The pain in his eyes as he looked down at her stopped her from asking any more. 'I'm sorry.' She took off her mask, not wanting to shield her face from him in that moment. 'It's…complicated. All of this is complicated.'

'Ash, it's fine, honestly…'

*All of what?*

He was still staring at her. His eyes, those beautiful eyes, so unique. She couldn't stop trying to fathom their depths. The pain behind them was something she recognised; she knew it. She recognised something in him. Was that what this was? This…this… thing between them?

*He's right. This is complicated.*

The rest of her words evaporated from her brain, the heat from the dancing and the proximity of Ash turning every solid thought into mush the second it was formed. His eyes were locked onto hers, and they were closer. Almost touching. Marnie didn't even know whose feet had moved. Everything but his gaze felt irrelevant as she looked right back. Seeing more than pain etched on his pupils the longer she looked. He took a deep shuddering breath in, and she couldn't stop her fingers from moving any longer. She reached up to Ash's face, slowly pulling the mask away from his features. He didn't move an inch, but she felt his hot sweet breath on her cheek as she touched the skin on his temple. She wanted to see his whole face.

'That's better,' she whispered. His lips twitched, and her eyes feasted on the movement. He dipped his head low, and she lifted herself towards him. The second their lips met, the crack of thunder they both felt pushed the two of them closer together. He wrapped his arms around her waist, pulling her up and against his strong body. She could feel his hands shaking as he held her close. His lips were sealed to hers, the pain she'd seen in his eyes moments earlier gone. There was no pain in Ash now, he was right there with her. She felt sexy when he looked at her.

Like a man starved. He twined his tongue with hers, deepening the kiss just as much as she wanted him to. She had her hands on his face, pulling him to her while their masks hung from her fingers from their straps.

'Marnie,' he breathed, in between long, deep caresses of her lips. Marnie whimpered at that, liking the sound of her name on his lust-filled tongue. This was the hottest thing she'd ever done. It wasn't just the masks either, the setting. It was as if she wanted to jump him, right here, right now. She'd laughed at that part in movies before, but, man, she got it now. *Ding-ding-ding.* She was on fire for the man. Wishing she were back in her cottage, and not with ice cream.

The twinkling of the lights behind Ash's head lit him up like a halo from behind. She opened her eyes just to check he was there and found herself drawn to his closed lids. She was at a ball, dressed to the nines, kissing the hot midwife who was covering her maternity leave. He was leaving, and she was sworn off men. He was hiding something, something dark, she knew it. She had dark corners of her own heart, and her pain thrummed with his. She felt it, just as deep as the kisses he was giving her with everything he had. She was drunk on kissing his lips, feeling his tongue dip into her mouth, exploring her and gripping her ever tighter. His soft, large hands were wrapped around her. She felt no cold, no breeze from the sea. She just felt warm, and safe. Sexy and daring. Like her. Marnie had got her groove back…

'Woo-hoo!' a rather drunken voice sang out behind them, and Ash's eyes sprang open. For a second, they grew lazy again when they locked with hers. He tightened his fingers around her, securing her to him. As if he was excited to find her there when his lashes lifted.

She felt the stirring of lust again even

in her panic, and then the voice turned into voices. They sprang apart, Marnie grabbing her mask and throwing his into his waiting hands. As they put on their disguises, breathing heavy and hard, she heard Ash call her name just as the crowd drowned out his words. A few masked and rather sozzled party-leavers looked their way, Ash nodding awkwardly in their direction. Marnie took the turn of his head as her cue, and she ran off, towards the crowd. The spell had well and truly been broken. The coach was a pumpkin, and she was off like a shot. Not trusting herself to stay with him any longer. Embarrassed about being caught snogging in the bushes too. She had to stay living here after all. People talked to each other. Everyone loved a party story. She didn't want to be the subject of gossip. Not again. Heck, no.

'What have you done?' she chided herself under her breath. 'Dear Lord, Marnie! Get it together!' Her lips still felt white hot, swollen from Ash's attentions. Brushing at them, she still felt the tingle from his lips. She was surprised they weren't on fire, scorched from the crackle that flowed between them.

*Imagine if you'd had sex,* her horny brain spat out.

'Imagine? I nearly did…' she whispered back to the voice.

She was breathing hard, and she knew it was more than the running she was doing. She'd stopped only to throw off her heels and grab them, but she'd heard Ash call her name. More than once. She didn't turn around, she didn't stop till she was standing outside her parents' house, her hand on the doorbell. The whole journey there was a blur. There she was though, intact, deranged with the thought of what she'd just fled from, and still masked. She pulled it off her face as her mother opened the door. She twanged the elastic against the shell of her ear in her haste. Ignoring the sting, she painted on a smile.

'Hi, Mum, everything okay with Violet?'

Her mother was never one for missing a trick. Marnie knew she was rumbled the second her mother's brows knitted together. She never scowled, but the lowering of the brows was a sure-fire sign that she'd clocked something. Marnie continued her tactic of acting breezy and grinning like an idiot.

'Oh, fine—she went right off after her bottle. She's been good for her grandma as always. How was the ball?'

Marnie followed her into the house, eager to see her daughter again. She realised she'd forgotten about her that night, caught in the moment with Ash. She'd thought she'd feel guilty, but, surprisingly, she just felt like a woman who'd had a good night. Despite its complications. She didn't know how she would sleep though. Hot and sweaty probably, as her dreams no doubt would be.

'It was good. Fun. How's Violet been?'

'My granddaughter has been as good as gold as always. You've asked that twice since you walked in. I raised you, you know. I didn't do half bad either, I think.' Her eyes crinkled in the corners as she smiled. Her eyes were still searching though, like bloodhounds after a scent. Marnie hoped she didn't look too dishevelled.

'How was the ball?' Her mother reached forward to pluck a blade of grass from Marnie's hair. 'Looks like you might have had some fun.'

Marnie didn't look her in the eye. 'It was good, I said. Lots of fun.'

*Mostly in cosy darkened corners.*

She felt her body get hot under her dress all over again.

'Hmm, I can see that.' Her mother started putting everything back into the changing bag, a knowing smile on her face. 'Your cheeks are flushed.' She smiled, her eyes dancing with mirth as Marnie looked at her agog. And very red-faced. She was flushed right through to the neckline. She felt as if she might combust. 'And your hair looks like you were dragged through a bush.'

Marnie's open mouth was her mother's only answer. Not that she needed one. She was too busy laughing while she packed up Violet's things.

The clock was a rather annoying concept. Time too. The clocks all ticked on, heralding the seconds of your life ticking by. Hours that you could be sleeping in. Much-needed sleep. She was lying in a comfy bed, warm and cosy. Violet was asleep, and she had time to get some much-needed shut-eye.

Which sounded perfect. Easy. Rare, given her new status as a single mother. She punched the pillow, looking once more at the clock. Three minutes had elapsed.

Marnie sighed and flumped face down on the duvet. It was no use. She couldn't sleep. She'd half dozed off an hour ago, but the instant her lashes met she was back on that green. Back in Ash's arms. In the shadows, kissing him. Tasting him. Exploring more. Fearful that she wouldn't find it, and wary that she would. Pulling him closer to her as he reached for her just as desperately.

How the heck was a woman supposed to sleep when she'd got that on her mind? Especially after a very long dry spell, and a 'no man' rule that was cast iron. She could plead temporary insanity or blame it on the mask, but when she'd realised he'd reached for her, she'd forgotten his abrupt exit. That was the problem. As her regency romances would say, she quite forgot herself when in the presence of that certain gentleman. This wasn't a book though. It was barely a chapter.

He was living next door, doing her job, working with her friends. He was getting entwined into Carey Cove. Into her life. Kisses in the dark were not part of any plan she had. She needed to stop thinking about her hunky neighbour and keep it as normal as possible till he left. Then she'd be back at work, tired, busy, and raising her daughter. Just as she'd planned.

She looked at the clock once more. Another four minutes lost to thoughts of Ash and the million reasons why kissing him again was a good idea. She'd felt more than his touch that night, and she wondered what his pain was. Why was a man like that single and travelling? Commitment phobic? She didn't get that kind of read from him. After Oliver, her instincts were sharp on that score. Maybe her resolve wasn't quite as steadfast as she'd thought, given her dalliance, but her instincts were always at play. But then, there hadn't been anyone *since* Oliver. Her friends had tried and failed to get her to go on dates. She'd rather die than be on some dating site. She had no intention of running that gauntlet. She didn't want a man, and she didn't need one either. Violet was proof that her plan was worth it.

She'd gone through the IVF alone. The injections, the appointments, the surging hormones. She'd cried buckets inside rooms at work, overwrought with the surges going on in her body while she was trying to work and not think about babies. Which, of course, had been impossible. They had been in her face all day long. She loved it, but her own longing had made it much harder.

As if on cue, Violet woke up, letting her mother know she was hungry with a good healthy squawk. Her unmistakable feeding cries. Balm to her ears after reflecting on the days before she came to be.

'It's okay.' Marnie smiled, rubbing her tired but wide eyes as she went to feed her daughter. 'Mummy's here.'

Once Violet was happily in her arms

feeding, Marnie's attentions turned back to Ash. She could see a light on upstairs at his place, and she wondered whether he was restless too.

*Are you thinking about me? I can't get you out of my head.*

She'd felt it when they'd worked on the decorations together. Brushing her hands against his, seeing his reaction. She knew he felt it. How could he not? It was all she could do sometimes to stay on her feet when he was close. Her whole body reacted to him instinctively. She'd never felt that with Oliver. Which made her wonder what she was in for.

She wasn't the type to go lusting after anyone. She didn't have the time or the patience for games. Or lies. Oliver had tested every limit on that score, and his betrayal was not something she was ever going to go running towards. She felt as if she'd been blindsided by him, and she was furious at the lies, the time wasted.

She felt the old anger and hurt rise

within her, Violet picking up on it and wriggling. Marnie shushed her and pushed Oliver back where he belonged in her brain. Firmly in the waste basket labelled 'trash'. Which was where she'd placed all *other* men, if she was honest. The only male she had wanted to have any truck with was Violet's sperm donor, and that wasn't a man per se. More of a strong sample in a jar. That was enough for her. No pain, no games, or lies.

And now she was lusting after her neighbour. He was passionate about the job, just like her. Her friends had kept her up to speed on his work, and they were impressed. Not an easy feat with the ladies of Carey House. He'd got the seal of approval. The thought made her smile through her fatigue. As she looked out of the window at Ash's lit window, she thought of something else.

His masked eyes at the ball, so full of something dark, hidden. She recognised it as pain. She'd seen it in the mirror enough times after her own difficult time. Pre Violet. He looked as if he was in need of sleep, pretty much all the time. Even at the ball she'd noticed how drawn he looked. It made her want to look after him. She was like that with everyone. It was her nature. Ash was different though. She recognised that. She wanted to know more, to help him even. It could be anything.

As she burped Violet and settled her back into her cot, she turned off the light and hoped that sleep would take her. She wanted to stop thinking about it. Ash could have any number of reasons for who and how he was. She didn't need to drive herself mad with all the best- and worst-case scenarios. It was dangerous on two counts. Once she knew, she would have to deal with it. The easy way out was just not to know. Not to get involved. Because, as Marnie tried to close her eyes and not think of the man whose lips she craved, she knew. The second count was him, and how he made her feel. There would be no coming back from that loss. It was far better to keep her head down and just keep her feelings to herself. He would be gone soon, and the feelings would pass. She hoped for that as much as she did for sleep.

Turning over, she looked out of the window into the night. The curtains were half closed, leaving a nice gap for her to focus on. It was Christmas, she had the engagement party to look forward to. It was also Violet's first Christmas, and the time when all their family traditions could be formed. She did think that it would have been nice to have Ash around, but she knew it would just get her in deeper. She had the life she had wanted for so long. Sure, it would have been nice to have someone to share it with, but life wasn't perfect. What she had was enough before Ash arrived. She lied herself to sleep. It would have to be enough. It was the plan, and she always stuck to the plan. Whatever Ash's deal was, it was for the next woman he kissed to worry about. In the next place.

It was another two hours before Marnie eventually slept, but she still dreamed of Ash. Driving away from Carey House, as Marnie watched from the doorway.

## CHAPTER SEVEN

'WOW, YOU LOOK how I feel.'

Marnie paused mid yawn. She had one hand on the doorframe, and the other scratching the mass of bed-head blonde hair on her head.

'Oh, cheers. Good morning to you too. Come on in.' She rolled her eyes theatrically at her friend, and moved aside to let Daisy in. She was rather weighed down with the big quilted black coat she was wearing, and she waddled like a duck through to the kitchen. Her fur-lined winter boots had a frosting of snow on their tops, and she smiled sheepishly.

'Sorry. For the snow and the snark.'

Marnie laughed, pulling out one of the chairs and helping her friend settle into it. Flicking the kettle on, she grabbed two mugs from the cupboard and checked the baby monitor. Violet was still flat out on the playmat, looking up at the jungle gym above her. Marnie smiled at the sight, and, making the tea, let her friend vent. 'It's fine. Come on, tell me.'

'I'm just so fed up,' Daisy moaned. 'I've drunk all the raspberry-leaf tea I can stomach; we had a vindaloo the other night. I've been on a million walks, till the snow stopped me. And I'm a nightmare to everyone. I just want to snap everyone's head off. Braxton Hicks are the worst.'

Marnie put a mug of tea in front of her and took a seat. After one look at Daisy's glum face, she got the biscuits out too. Daisy threw her a look of pure guilt.

'I'm sorry. You're the last person I should be moaning to.'

'Give over, and moan away. I get it.'

'I know, but with everything you went through…'

Marnie's hand was on hers before the sentence was finished.

'Listen, we all have our own journeys to motherhood. Every journey is hard, no matter what road's taken. You're three days overdue in your pregnancy! You're tired, excited, nervous. You want to meet your baby. There isn't a woman in the world who wouldn't feel a bit down.'

Daisy smiled, through watery eyes. 'I knew you'd get it. It's worth it though, right?' Daisy looked across at Violet. Marnie followed her gaze, her whole face lighting up.

'It's the best.' She smiled back at her friend and squeezed her fingers tight. 'You moan away, have a biscuit. I'll go find a film.'

Daisy grinned, happy to be distracted. 'Popcorn?'

Marnie winked. 'You know it!' She looked through the movies with the remote, settling on a funny rom-com they'd both watched before and loved.

* * *

Marnie was putting a load of washing on when she heard Daisy from the lounge.

'Ooh!'

'Daisy? You okay?'

She half ran to the lounge, but Daisy was still on the couch, Marnie's ball mask hanging from her fingertips.

'Yeah, I forgot about the ball! How did it go?'

Marnie tutted. 'Daisy, I thought the baby was coming then! It was good. Great.'

Daisy shook her head. 'Listen, your daughter can listen to this conversation and not even know it, so spill.' Daisy was smirking now. Teasing.

*Oh, crumbs.*

Marnie's jaw dropped.

*Gosh, did everyone know what was going on? Was it her face, giving her away? Were people talking? Oh, no.*

'What do you mean?' She feigned ignorance but gave up when she realised Daisy wasn't buying it. It had been a pretty poor attempt. She couldn't help it but whenever she thought of Ash, even though she couldn't do anything about her attraction to him long term, she knew she lit up. It was driving her crazy, but she smiled at her friend and hoped she'd at least buy that. 'You're being weird.'

Daisy laughed. 'Yeah, I'm being weird.' She air-quoted her sentence, the epitome of sarcasm between the two of them. 'I saw you, dancing with that guy! You know, tall, dark? Wearing a mask? Who was he?'

'Oh, him.' She waved her away. 'Just a father of one of the babies I delivered.' She groaned. Wow, that was pathetic. Thinking on the spot was normally her forte, but Ash made her mumble, blurt things out awkwardly.

*I think I'm in trouble. Hormones! It's the hormones, calm yourself.*

Thinking of being twirled in Ash's arms under the Christmas lights. The heat of his body against hers…

'Marnie! Hello?'

Marnie snapped her eyes to the impatient bloodhound before her. 'What?'

'I have never seen you act like that around one of the new dads before.' Daisy's smile was near smug, and Marnie blushed. 'Well, I'm sure I'll get it out of you.' She looked sincere. 'I'm glad for you, either way. You looked like you were having fun.'

Marnie didn't say anything, just busied herself with setting them both up for the film. It was a distraction tactic, of course, but it worked. Daisy was in need of a sit and a bit of girl time, and she happily let the subject drop in favour of sweet popcorn and a bit of Christmas cake. Marnie had done nothing but bake Christmas cake and cookies when she couldn't sleep waiting for Violet to come. Daisy could enjoy the fruits of her labour, so to speak. The thought made her smile.

She sliced some cheese to add to the slices of rich fruitcake, marzipan and royal icing before heading back to her friend. She was glad Daisy had come to visit. It was better than the two women spending the morning alone in their homes. They both needed something to keep them busy, albeit for very different reasons. Marnie found she really needed this too. As distraction techniques went, this one wasn't half bad for her either. It stopped her from thinking about that kiss, the jolt she felt when she was around Ash. She'd never felt like that with Oliver. She wondered now whether she would feel it with anyone else.

*No, stop it, Marnie! There is no man in your plan. Read the fine print. Career, home, baby. That's it.*

He was leaving anyway, and those eyes…

There was more to Ash than met the eye, and she knew it. That was half the problem, she guessed. Maybe she should just ask him outright. Maybe he was married, a total cad! Then all of this angst would be a moot point.

*Oh, dear Lord,* she thought to herself as she walked back to her friend. *You really need to get it together.*

One film turned into two, and the two women were having such fun. Daisy was more relaxed, and all baby and sexy colleague/neighbour frustrations were forgotten for the moment. Marnie was putting their plates in the dishwasher when she heard a sharp gasp behind her, followed by an unmistakably loud splash of liquid onto her kitchen tile.

'Marnie, I think the baby might be coming.'

'Really?' Marnie was shocked and excited at the same time. The excited friend had taken over from the seasoned midwife in her, and she'd not even moved.

'Er...yeah, my waters just broke on your floor.'

The two women looked down at the pool of liquid and back up to each other.

After a long second, Marnie sprang into action.

'Oh, okay. Baby coming! Right!'

Violet chose that moment to let out a lustful cry, and Marnie's training kicked in. She was going to need some help, and fast. She realised that she had it, right next door. She needed Ash. He picked up on the second ring.

'Marnie?'

'Yes, it's me, I—'

'Hi, listen, I'm glad you called—'

His voice was soft, and she wondered what he was going to say for half a second before Daisy let out another puff of air and a groan.

'I need you, Ash. Are you home? My friend's in labour!'

'What? Where are you?'

'At home—can you come?'

The line was silent for a half-second, and then his strong voice came through the line, as clear as a bell, even over the wails of Daisy and Violet.

'I'll be right there.'

He bounded through the front door, his kit bag in hand. Marnie, having quickly wiped up the spill on the kitchen floor, was just settling Daisy onto her sofa. She'd just put a new Christmas-themed throw on there. It wouldn't make it, but maybe her sofa would. She laid some towels down quickly and Ash headed to the kitchen. Marnie could hear him washing his hands in the sink as she settled Daisy as comfortably as possible.

'Have you rung work, let them know we have incoming?' Ash asked as he entered the room.

'I'll call now.' Marnie found the contact and fired off a quick call to Carey House. As ever, the staff were ready and willing to help, and by the time Marnie had hung up she knew they were organising transportation to get Daisy and her baby delivered there safely. She saw Ash watching her and turn to their patient the second he'd seen her looking. Marnie knelt down by Daisy at the foot of the couch.

'Hi, I'm Ash Ellerington.' He smiled easily at her friend, and Marnie was once again distracted by the smile on the man. When he flashed his pearly whites, she found herself utterly lost and incapable of speech.

*Trouble,* she reminded herself. Trouble was what this man meant. Chaos in the relative order of her life.

Daisy let out a low growl, which snapped Marnie back into the room.

'Hi,' Daisy said through gritted teeth. 'I would shake your hand, but…' Another contraction took hold, and they were coming faster. This baby wasn't going to wait for an ambulance. 'Argh!' She breathed through the latest contraction, Marnie timing it with her wristwatch. Once it passed, Daisy puffed out and relaxed against the cushions.

Ash laughed softly. He knelt down by Marnie's side, his leg jamming up against hers. A half-second later, she saw him jolt from the contact just as she felt it reverberate through her own body. She could feel the heat from his thigh warm her own. She resisted the urge to dry-hump his leg, given the situation, but only just. If there hadn't been a woman in imminent labour in the room, she had a feeling it would be a different matter. Ash was looking at her, his expression just as shocked as hers.

*Is he really feeling this like I am?*

Marnie felt as if the pair of them could burst into flames. Just as she was trying to focus back on her patient, he broke her gaze, and it was back to business.

'Don't worry, Daisy, is it?' Marnie nodded at him as she helped Daisy to remove her underclothes. Once Daisy was relatively comfortable, the frown on her face softened a little. She smiled at Marnie, before turning her gaze back to Ash. Marnie recognised her mischievous grin a mile off. Her friend might be in labour, but she still hadn't missed a trick. She wondered momentarily whether Daisy had seen the sparks between them.

'Yeah, that's right. Nice to meet you, Ash.' She waved her arms around her. 'Not in these circumstances, obviously.' She turned to look him up and down fully, and Marnie felt her whole body tense. He passed her a pair of gloves and she avoided looking at him as they both put theirs on. 'Settling into Carey Cove, okay?'

Daisy's face changed from curious to uncomfortable again, and Marnie thanked her contraction for being a distraction. She was still timing it when Daisy spoke again. 'Weird—' pant of breath '—without your—' pant of breath '—mask on? *Eee-yah-ah!*'

The question turned into more of a steam-kettle noise towards the end, but she knew Ash had understood every word by the blush on his cheeks. Marnie focused on the business end of her friend and chose to ignore the other situation altogether.

'Daisy, you're fully dilated already, okay. When you feel the urge to push, push!'

She took her friend's hand, ignoring the vice-like grip and breathing right along with her, Ash by her side. The two women panted together and in a few short contractions, Ash delivered the baby and placed him right on Daisy's chest. The little boy let out a lusty cry, and as Ash checked him over Marnie checked Daisy and marvelled at the moment she'd watched her friend become a mother.

'Oh, Daisy, he's perfect! Well done. He was fast for a first baby!' Ash's smile was so happy.

Daisy, her hair matted with sweat, pushed a lock away from her forehead and, tearful, she kissed the top of her new son's head.

'I'm so sorry about your living room!' She laughed, and Marnie brushed her off.

A tear fell down her own cheek as she laughed with her friend.

'Don't worry, he's worth it,' she retorted. 'You did good, Daisy. He's perfect. Ten digits, and ten toes.'

'Thanks, I'm even more glad I got bored at home this morning now.'

The two women laughed together as Ash dealt with the placenta, giving Daisy an injection to bring it along a little faster and clearing away the debris of the very fast home delivery. He watched the two women laugh together, Marnie's ruined sofa not even a thought in their heads. He'd witnessed something special today. Something different. It felt more personal. Being here, in Marnie's home, with her assisting the delivery right next to him.

Birthing babies was always special, but watching Marnie do it, with her friend as the patient, that was something else. His heart was breaking wide open, and that wasn't a good thing. Even just then, back there, touching her body with his had reminded him of how she made him feel. How he felt when he was around her. He'd never expected to feel anything like that again, but this woman, the feelings he experienced with her…and it was with her, he knew that.

As he left the two women to clean up, and enjoy the moment, he washed up in the kitchen and put the rest of his kit back into the bag he'd brought. All the while thinking of how Marnie's lips parted whenever she first saw him. As though a breath had caught in her throat, and she needed air back in her lungs. How he felt when he was near—

The horn sounded outside. The transport to Carey House had arrived. Zipping his bag up, he pushed the thoughts away and headed out of the cottage to meet the team outside. Relay the happy news of the birth and all that it entailed. Well, almost all.

## CHAPTER EIGHT

MARNIE CLOSED HER front door, giving herself a minute before she turned back to the hallway. When she did, Ash was standing there, kit bag on his shoulder.

'Well, that was quite a morning. I can't believe Violet slept through the whole thing.'

Ash's gaze turned towards the sitting room, where Violet was snoring in her baby chair. She'd kicked up a fuss in the beginning but had nodded off just as things had got going.

'Well, I think she takes after her mother.' Ash's voice was husky. Like a dark whisper. It reached more than her ears and made a reaction. 'Nothing much seems to faze you, does it?'

Marnie laughed, mentally brushing off

his words as much as her heart clung to them. 'Well, it's part of the job, isn't it?'

Ash put his kit bag down. It made a thud by his feet. 'I wasn't talking about the job. You're someone to watch, Marnie Richards.' He looked down at the hallway floor, as if deciding something. He bit at his lip, and Marnie felt that jolt once more.

*He's not even touching me. Yet.*

'I can't stop watching you. It's driving me mad.'

Somewhere between the biting of his lip and the words he spoke after, Marnie had found herself an inch from him, and his arms reached for her as if he couldn't bear to not touch her for a second longer.

'Me too.' That was all she could get out before they smashed against each other, groin to groin, her leg flying around his. He grabbed it with a steady hand and lifted her up, tighter against him. Holding her legs around him, he kissed at her neck hungrily before moaning in impatience. Marnie clawed at his back, pulling him tighter towards her as her back hit the wall. His arms were wrapped round her, his hand now grabbing her bottom. He dipped his head and kissed her again. Kissed her as if he'd been waiting years to do it. She ran her fingers up through his hair, ruffling it and feeling it flow over her fingertips.

*God, he was sexy. She was desperate for more, for him. She'd never get enough.*

'Marnie,' he breathed. 'Do you feel that?' He looked half mad with curiosity; his eyes boring into her up close. Now given that Marnie could feel how aroused he was against her, she could have answered with something cheeky, but she didn't. She knew what he was talking about. The attraction, the jolt.

'The thunderbolt?' She asked him out loud, and his face sparked with recognition as he took her lips with his again. He kissed her as though he wished to do nothing else for the foreseeable. As if he couldn't believe it was happening, and he wasn't going to waste a second of it. It was all very intoxicating. She couldn't get close enough to him, get enough of his huge, splayed palms spread across her backside. She rubbed mercilessly against him before realising what she was doing. She stopped, and his hands pulled her closer, him moving her body closer himself as he growled into her neck.

'Tell me about the thunderbolt,' he demanded rather than asked. What was it about Ash when they got closer? He turned into some kind of grizzled, husky mountain man. She absolutely couldn't get enough of it. She was still in his arms, tight in her hallway, pushed against the wall. Against him. When he pulled his head back to look at her, she was struck once more by the sheer beauty of his hazel eyes. She'd never look at another pair of eyes the same, not after his.

'It makes me crazy,' she admitted, and

his lazy, satisfied smile made her insides turn to goo.

'Me too,' he said, dipping his head to kiss the tip of her chin. He didn't release his hands but hers were all over him. In his hair, touching the lines of his chest through his thin cotton T-shirt. 'What else?'

She reached to kiss him, but he pulled away, just a touch. She hummed at his denial, and he laughed. 'Tell me what you feel, and I'll kiss you more.' His eyes were half closed, hazy. He was as turned on as she was. She raised a brow at him and lifted the corners of his T-shirt up. Showing off a glimpse of his bare, chiselled chest in the warm light of the cottage.

'I feel abs,' she breathed as she ran her fingertips down the patch of skin she'd uncovered. Discovered more like. She felt like an adventurer, up here in his arms. She might as well be sitting on a table. She would be just as safe. Well, not quite.

As turned on as she was, she couldn't deny how protected he made her feel, too. As if she were the only woman in the world that mattered to him. It was a rather heady emotion. No wonder the sparks had come. It was as if their energy had nowhere else to go but just zapped between them in frustration. She'd thought… well…

'Marnie,' he said, his face dipping into a frown. He looked concerned, and he was still breathing hard. She realised her hands were still in his hair, but she'd been miles away. In her own head.

'Marnie.'

This time, her eyes snapped back fully to his. His voice was stronger, more passionate, more…commanding. 'Are you still with me?'

His face had moved closer with each word, and she could feel the brush of his bottom lip against hers, then it was gone. Just half an inch away. Half a zap of lightning flashed between them, the prospect of what came next scary, but, oh…my…gosh. It would be…amazing.

# CHAPTER NINE

*HAVE I LOST this moment?*

That was running on replay in Ash's mind as his arms still clung to her gorgeous body.

*I'm so turned on, please don't stop this.*

He knew he should be remembering something, that he should be staying away. He was so drunk on this woman, this amazing woman who didn't need anyone but made him want to protect her like some bear of a man from the Dark Ages—it was something he just couldn't shake. He was starting to dread the day he'd leave this place. The thing was, he'd kind of figured that out before now. His mind didn't drift, hadn't drifted. He was right here, in this moment and loving every minute of it.

'Marnie,' he said again, his voice sounding deep and broken, even for him. 'You with me?' He tried not to, but he touched his lips to hers. Just for a second, or five. He had to, he thought he might explode otherwise. It didn't help when she moaned in response.

*Wow. I want to make her do that again. A lot.*

The thing she did next was nearly the ending of him. He nearly dropped her on the stop. She answered him.

'Yes, Ash.' She brushed her lips against his, licking at them playfully when she pulled away. 'I'm with you.'

He smiled, and he wanted to say something else. A lot of things, some things that would definitely kill the moment and how he was feeling holding his own little spark of light in his arms. That was what she was, he thought as their lips came together again, their bodies pushing against each other to get closer.

*She's a spark of light. A bolt I didn't ex-*

*pect, clear out of the Cornish blue sky. A star lit up on the Christmas tree.*

So he was glad he didn't say anything. He didn't want to do anything, say anything to break their bubble. He wanted more of her. So he didn't make a sound. Someone did though. Violet.

His hand was on the outside of Marnie's underwear when Violet woke up. And, boy, did she wake up. Marnie's face dropped, and she wiggled out of his arms. He stayed her movements and placed her back down on the floor. She looked at him for a long moment, but he couldn't make out whether her expression was one of disappointment, or guilt. Or panic. She seemed to put a mask on the second her daughter alerted her. He felt foolish maybe, reckless, sure, but not guilty. That would imply that he regretted it. He felt more as if her dad had just walked in on them kissing in her bedroom.

'I, er…sorry.'

She was back, Violet in her arms now.

The little one was teary-eyed and clearly still tired. It was only then that he noticed the tiredness was etched on her mother's face too.

'Let me guess.' He walked across to them. Violet observed him with features just like the woman holding her. He smiled at them both before answering. He felt as though he needed a moment to get over the sight of the two of them.

Was that it? Was that why he was attracted to her? A single woman with a newborn baby? No, he already knew he'd questioned that before. Without even quite knowing why. Well, he did know why. The first time they'd met, in the waiting room at Carey House. Wow, he'd thought he was going to pass out right in front of her that day. He knew he'd not even noticed her baby, or even thought about why a woman like that might be in the room. He'd just clocked her. Her questioning, curious eyes. Her sleek blonde bob, severe-looking on most people, but on her it just made her look fiercely beautiful. Especially now, he thought with a curl of his lip. 'She didn't sleep last night.'

Marnie shook her head. 'Nope. She just needs her nappy changing. I'll just take her up…'

'Oh, okay.' He took a step back in the hallway. 'Do you want me to go, let you…?'

He stopped talking when she met his eye. 'Can you stay?'

His nod was all he could get out without saying something sappy. Her returning smile nearly took him to his knees. He watched her carry her child up the stairs of the house that mirrored his in everything from size to layout but not in heart. This place was a real home. It reeked of Marnie, and Violet was everywhere now. Not in a hoarder kind of way, but just in the way a proud mother would want. Photos in frames, toy box ready in the lounge. Play mat out, bottles in the steriliser. Everything neatly stacked, in order, in the kitchen, he noticed as he looked around a little, walking slowly and taking in every detail.

He could make out Marnie's voice from upstairs. She was humming something about being over a rainbow, and it made him smile, but his heart clench. It wasn't because she was a mother. It was because of her.

He looked around the rest of the kitchen. It was neat, everywhere really. You could tell she was a new mother, of course, but he could tell she cleaned a lot. He did the same. He wondered whether she did it out of boredom too. Something to chase the feelings away.

He focused on the fridge, which was adorned with orderly photos weighed down by fridge magnets from places all around. She must have travelled at some point. Before settling down in her home town and raising a family. He was still travelling, and still carrying baggage. He felt his shoulders sag. This was messy, and he didn't want to hurt her. That was the last thing he wanted. The first thing was more of what they'd just done in the hallway.

He wanted to do more hallway stuff. Boy, did he, but it came with conversations, and talking. Longing and counting down days on his rota. Till the last day. When he would do what? Just leave and go to the next job, as if nothing had happened? He didn't relish any part of that in his future. He didn't have a plan, as such. He knew if he had, though, it wouldn't have included this. He'd met a woman like Marnie at a time that he wasn't looking or expecting to. Or wanting to, for that matter. He realised that his heart wasn't quite the swinging brick he'd thought it was now. The fast beating of his heart was testament to how strong that organ was at the moment. Half thudding out of his chest.

He heard the humming stop, and her footsteps on the stairs. This was it. This was the perfect time to escape again. He should just leave and avoid her for the rest of his time. He could do that at work, even though everything about Carey House seemed to remind him of her. She was part of the place, as noticeable as the paint covering the walls. He could take extra shifts if they came up. Bury himself in work for a different reason than normal. A less sad one, but still, a situation still best avoided.

He should contact the agency, ask them to replace him. He would be sent elsewhere. Something had stopped him though. He told himself it was because he'd already been two weeks late to start. He didn't like to let people down, and the staff at Carey House didn't deserve to be left in the lurch. He didn't want to upset Marnie either. She would probably blame herself, for not being there. Nya said that she would probably come back before the end of her proposed maternity leave. Maybe after the festivities were over, she would want to come back. Then all of this angst would be for nothing. He could stick it out another couple of weeks.

He'd been planning to ask to work over Christmas anyway. It wouldn't be any different to do that here. It would be easy. He could keep his head down, hide out in his cottage. Wait his time out. It sounded like a plan. A plan that had one question attached to it that he couldn't work out the answer to for the life of him. The question was why wasn't he heading right out of the front door? He had his keys in his hand, but his feet didn't move.

## CHAPTER TEN

ALL THE TIME she was upstairs, soothing her very cranky and very tired baby back off to sleep, she was thinking of what came next. When Violet's soothed mood and now dry nappy lulled her back to sleep, and Marnie faced Ash again.

Thankfully, her baby daughter seemed to get the gravity of the situation and dropped right back off to sleep. Perhaps the totally sleepless night she'd endured had a good reason after all.

She half ran to the mirror to check her appearance, but she was oddly thrilled by what she saw. She looked drawn, sure, but she also looked like a woman she'd not seen in a while. A rather happy one with a blushing complexion. It was heady, spending time around Ash. Addictive perhaps.

She'd already spent some time daydreaming about what it would be like working with him at Carey House. How he'd looked in the waiting room haunted her. It would feel weird now for her to be there and not see him somehow. Her friends had spent the energy of many texts and calls telling her how well he was already doing filling in for her. How attentive he was, how good he was with the patients, and the team. He'd already won the girls over, Marnie could tell. They didn't say anything about a personal life though.

She quickly slipped on some strawberry-flavoured lip gloss, something she did when she felt a little on edge. It gave her confidence without looking too flirty. She straightened up her sleek bob, untangling the curls Ash had woven in with his touch. His lip on her ear, driving her mad enough that she'd lost the power of speech. It was as if time had stopped, but then Violet had stepped in. She knew she should feel guilty, but she was a single mum in every sense of the word. There was no father to hurt in this scenario. She was the sole parent to her daughter, and she was entitled to a life too. She didn't want to just be a midwife and mother, by any means.

Once she was looking more like herself, if a little tired and sparkly eyed, she checked on a sleeping Violet and headed back down the stairs. Ash wasn't in the kitchen, and her heart near stopped when she considered the fact that he might be sitting next door. Wondering how the hell he was going to get out of the situation he'd just walked and nuzzled and kissed himself into.

She turned towards the lounge and stopped in the doorway. He was sitting on the couch, legs spread apart, looking comfortable and huge on her sofa. He looked up when she walked in, his face changing from a pensive look to a wide smile.

'She went back down okay?' He stood and crossed the room. His hand was in hers and she was sitting next to him on the sofa before she could utter a word.

'Yeah, fine. She needs the sleep, although it might cost me later.'

He chuckled softly, but then it died in his throat. 'Marnie, I don't want to complicate your life in any way.'

Marnie turned to look at him before she answered. She wanted to gauge the tone of his words by the expression on his face, but he gave nothing away. She played it safe.

'Well, I think that you saved me today. With Daisy. I needed the help.' Her face dropped when she realised she was sitting on said couch, but she had taken the covers off the cushions and covered them over with a new throw. He followed her gaze and laughed again. Once more, it didn't last long.

'I don't want to hurt you, Marn.'

*Marn?* No one had ever called her that. It sounded amazing coming from his mouth, but she concentrated on keeping her own face expressionless. Like his. He was giving something away though. His pain. It was there in his eyes. She knew it as she knew her own. She let him keep talking.

'I was married once.' She wasn't expecting him to say that, but at least she knew now. She could process it. He must have seen her facial expression. He held up his hands as if in surrender, his hazel eyes focused solely on her.

'I'm single now, but I don't stay in one place. My job is covering for you. When you go back to work, that will be the end of…it.'

'I know. I've always known that, of course. I wasn't expecting this, but it doesn't change my plans.'

He took her hand in his, and that stopped her train of thought.

'Plans?' he asked, his thumb rubbing soft, slow circles across the back of her hand. It was very…distracting. Not annoying distracting, but harder to get her words out. And mean them.

'Yes…er…plans. As you already know, I had Violet through IVF using a donor, so I don't need a father for my child. I knew what the deal was, and I was more than happy with that.' She frowned at her use of the past tense. He tongue-tied her when he was this close. 'I am happy with that. I don't plan on being in a relationship.' Ash was looking at her intently, and it was the first crack in his mask. He looked disappointed. She was sure she'd seen it on his face before he looked away. When he looked back and locked her eyes down with his hazel orbs, his face was all business once more.

'That's that, then, we know where we stand.' They both nodded numbly at each other. He cocked his head. 'Why were you single, can I ask? Before your plan started.'

She sighed, remembering the details and feeling bored of the whole thing. And stung with shame too. Not as bad as before, but it still pained her to speak of it. She knew it had worked out for the best, but rising like a phoenix didn't mean that the ashes didn't still throw an ember of memory out from time to time. It still stung, that feeling of being so utterly betrayed by the one person she trusted the most. Now, she was free of it, she reminded herself.

'I wasn't, at least, not for that long anyway. I was engaged.'

His hand stuttered for just a second, but the circles continued. She half expected to see little blue sparks when she looked down at their hands, but it was just his huge hand covering hers. 'He broke it off just as we were about to get married. It was very public, and messy, and hurtful. I was humiliated and I didn't even see it coming.' She smiled when she made another comparison she probably shouldn't. 'A bit like you coming along.' His eyes focused on hers then. 'In a good way.'

'In a good way?' he checked; his brow raised. His hand started to move a little faster.

'Yeah, I think so. I know you said you used to be married, but…'

His hand stopped then. 'That has nothing to do with you though, it just means that I like to move around. I need it, I guess.' She nodded in understanding. She'd taken a good look at her life after Oliver and decided to take the plunge with what she wanted in life. Hers had just meant staying close to home. He wanted to be out in the world. Maybe that was what the sparks were about. Maybe he was just an interlude in her life. One that she needed to finally free her of Oliver and the stain he seemed to have left on her ability to care about men. At all.

'We're on the same page, as clichéd as it

is. I don't want a relationship or a daddy for my baby, you don't want anything serious, and you're leaving anyway.' The look on his face told her that she'd laid it all out there rather bluntly. 'Sorry.'

'No,' he said a little bit too slowly. 'I get it. You have your life, and I have mine.'

'And a shelf life,' she agreed. She felt a little sad about that, but she didn't pick it apart in that moment. She could think about it later, digest it when Ash had left Carey Cove, and she was back fully into her new life. A working mum, just as she'd planned. That would be enough to juggle for anyone. She had no time for a man. Even one who looked like Ash. Who pulled her close as she was thinking of reasons to pull apart from him. From the touch she relished every time. The touch that made her body flicker into life. She went willingly, and they lay on the sofa together for the longest time. Holding each other in the quiet of the room and enjoying every moment. It was only minutes, but she thought of everything they could and couldn't be to each other. When she looked up at him, she knew he was contemplating it himself.

'It is a shame though,' she said out into the room. 'Another life, eh?'

'I just don't want to hurt you.' His chest rumbled his words through her, and she relished every single one, even if they contained twinges of something akin to pain too. 'I'm not here for ever—'

'I know.' She cut him off. He looked so stricken, and she needed him to know that it wasn't one-sided. She wasn't some lovesick teenager, hanging on his every word. She was a grown woman. He was the distraction in her plan, not part of it. She'd be just fine after Ash. She was before, right?

'Listen, we don't have to keep torturing each other like this. You were married, I was almost married. It's not like either one of us wants to run back down the aisle. You're leaving, and I have my job to go back to, and Violet to raise. After Oliver, I promised myself I would never be in that position again.'

Just thinking about it now angered her. The humiliation, the betrayal was bad enough. It wasn't that that gave her pause though. It was the fact that it meant that she'd never really known Oliver at all. That was what irked her the most. The fact that the man she'd chosen to spend her life with was an illusion. The Oliver in her head was not the Oliver she'd been due to walk down the aisle with and she wasn't in a hurry to make a mistake like that ever again. 'Listen, I have my own plan for my life, with Violet. I never had a man figure in it. I wasn't expecting you.'

'I wasn't expecting you either.' He didn't look completely unhappy at the thought.

*Good, I don't regret it either.*

'We're both on the same page, as rubbish as the book might be.'

'Exactly. Hey, if our exes could see us

now. I wonder what they would think about how much they messed us up.'

'Yeah, well.' Ash let go of her to run a hand through his already ruffled hair. 'If you ask me, Oliver is an idiot. You had a lucky escape. He didn't deserve you.'

'I have to agree with you there.' Marnie laughed softly. His jaw was tensed when she finally looked across at him. He was mad, brooding.

'I mean it. He's a jerk, hurting you like that.' He filled her eyesight, her senses, with those hazel eyes she'd come to love seeing day after day. 'I don't want to ever hurt you like that. I could never…'

She silenced him by doing what she felt. She kissed him. He wasn't a jot like Oliver. She didn't know much about Ash, or his story before Carey Cove, but she knew that much. He didn't have Oliver's arrogance, for a start. She felt as though she could trust him. He'd always been so different from Oliver, even if she'd been blind or too reluctant to see it when she'd first met him. As she kissed him, telling him everything with her tongue, she decided to just enjoy the moment. She'd have Christmas with him, surely that would be enough?

'Marnie.' Ash pulled away. Just enough to break their lips apart, but his arms came up around her. Encircling her in his grasp. She could smell the fabric softener on his clothing, the aftershave emanating from his delicious neck. His eyes were half closed when he focused on her once more. 'What are we doing? I thought we agreed to…' His words trailed off, his grip tightening. 'I don't think I can stay away from you. While I'm here, I—'

'Want to spend every minute with me?' she finished for him. He nodded, his expression hopeful, unguarded. She reached for him, tighter. One hand came up around his side, slowly brushing each finger along the confines of his clothing. He drew a ragged breath when her finger came up to brush his lips. 'I don't want to be away from you either. We have Christmas, right? I'm good with that.'

And she was. Whatever came after, she would remember her time with this heavenly man. Fondly, she hoped. And not wistfully. She didn't want Ash Ellerington to be something else she would have to survive through. Even if she knew every moment together would be worth it, his departure was ever looming between them. Of course, right now, in his arms, she was finding it hard to remember that fact. The thought of him being anywhere but here, right now, was more than she was willing to think about. For tonight, the plan was in the kitchen drawer of her mind. Something to be picked up and dealt with later. For now, on this snowy December afternoon, Marnie was choosing to live in the moment.

# CHAPTER ELEVEN

SHE WAS OFFERING him herself, and Christmas together. Violet was still sleeping, but he knew she would be a part of the picture too. They came as a package deal. If he spent more time with Marnie, then Violet would be there too, of course. He knew that. He was well aware of her plan, and how important her daughter was to her. That little girl was the centre of her universe, and he'd known that from their first meeting.

He'd seen a lot of mothers over the years. Growing up with sisters, he was pretty in tune with the female brain, and how it worked. Add motherhood to that, and the woman changed. Whether she expected to or not. Some mothers were overwhelmed, which he understood.

When he'd thought of being a father, he'd felt the weight of responsibility as well as the joy. Marnie was here doing everything on her own. He was in awe of her, and the thought of tainting it should have rung like an alarm bell in his head, but all he felt was happiness at the thought of spending time with Marnie, with both of them.

He shuddered as her finger continued its travels along his lips, and he felt it deep in his…well, trousers. This woman, even just having given birth and cared for a child single-handedly mere weeks ago, was gorgeous. Her curves were in all the right places, she had the best shock of blonde hair in a haircut that drew him to his knees. That time they'd kissed, and he'd run his hands through her hair, wow. That night all he could think about in bed was how sexy she'd looked with her hair all messed up. *By me.* He told her that, minus the territorial comment. He did feel protective of her though. He wanted this to be a good experience for both of them. In all ways. If it was going his way.

'I think we should go upstairs,' she said, as if she'd plucked the thoughts right out of his head.

'Okay,' was all he could croak in response. Marnie picked up the baby monitor and took his hand. He was out of the arms of that couch and into hers in half a second, and he drew her to him. Lifting her. She wrapped her legs around him, giggling into his neck.

'Sorry,' she started, but he shook his head. The smile he threw her probably gave too much of himself away, but he was out of breath. Not from carrying her, he was meant to do that. He could feel the jolt between them, pulsating the more they touched. Out of breath from looking at her. He dropped a kiss on her lips and headed for the stairs. She pushed open her bedroom door with her dangling foot, and Ash walked right over to the bed and sat down. Her knees brushed the surface of the duvet, and she clenched her legs around him.

'Don't panic,' he said softly, aware that her eyes had widened when they hit the bed. 'We don't have to do anything.'

She blushed, her eyes falling to his lips before she met his gaze again.

'I want to, it's just…been a while.' She rolled her eyes, a comical grimace crossing her features that he'd never seen before. 'Oliver.'

He felt his throat constrict and swallowed hard. 'I understand. It's been a while for me too.'

She waited for him to elaborate; he could see it. It took him a moment to get the voice to answer.

'My wife.'

*Oh, God, don't ask me to tell you any more. I can't bear it. Not now.*

She nodded slowly. 'We're in the same boat, then.'

He relaxed when she smiled at him, her eyes on his lips again. The mood was far from broken, but it took him a moment to focus again. He was close on that one. It was getting harder now not to have the conversation, but after her comments on the single-mother thing, it wasn't the time. He couldn't break this moment if he tried. He would probably be struck by lightning the second he walked out of the front door.

'I have something else to tell you.' She was biting her lip now. He braced himself for what she had to say. It would take a lot for him to leave. Probably the house caving in wouldn't stop him. He was enjoying being with her too much, even with the secrets and the inner torture of opening up his heart, his life, even to another person. Even temporarily. He was never the love-and-leave-them kind of man, and he didn't relish starting now. Especially not with the woman currently sitting astride him. 'I just had a baby.'

He laughed, part relief, part loving her

sense of humour. 'Marn, I am aware of that fact. A Carey-House-delivered baby.'

Marnie smiled. He knew about her birth story. Her girls at work had been meddling, he could feel it. Oh, they hadn't revealed any patient details, but he knew them well enough to know them to be a very romantic bunch. No matter what they might have protested. Nya was the worst meddler, but she had a heart of gold that even outshone the rest of the team of angels he worked with. They adored Marnie, and he could see why. In about fifty different ways. Just off the top of his head.

'That's right, I'm just saying. I have a new mum body.' He laughed again, but her look stopped it.

'Oh, come on.' He shook his head, and caught her chin in his grasp. He kissed her once, twice. The third time because he couldn't resist, even though he wanted to get his words out. 'You are breathtaking, Marnie. I really fancy you.'

She smirked then, and he rolled his eyes. 'I sound about twelve.'

'No.' Marnie shook her head softly. 'I really fancy you too.'

There was no more talking for a while. Marnie slowly undressed Ash, as he undressed her. They stood together, taking each other in for a long moment before coming back together on top of the covers. They wanted to take their time, but, with Violet to think about, Ash knew that this time would never be enough. He would want more, even before he'd had it.

They kissed and explored each other, running fingers along each other's skin and learning the maps of each other. He wondered for a moment how it would feel when it came time to leave, but she reached for him then, and the thought floated right out of his head. Reaching for his wallet from his trouser pocket, he pulled out a condom. She lay beneath him, her hair messed up and wild across the sheets around her head. She was stunning, and it took him a second to gather himself before he lowered his lips back to hers. He lined himself up, her gasp as he pushed against her opening driving him wild. He didn't push any further, choosing instead to kiss her some more. He couldn't get enough of kissing this woman.

She wiggled her hips beneath him, and his resolve was broken. He slid in slowly, giving her a chance to adjust to him. The second he pushed in, they gasped together, his groan a low rumble that skipped across her chest. Her hands were in his hair as he rocked against her, slowly, languidly at first, but then harder, faster. She moved with him. He was enjoying every second and wanting to kiss her lips clean off her face. He grunted when she moved slightly beneath him, taking him in further.

'Slow down,' he urged. 'I don't want this feeling to stop.' He never wanted this feeling to stop. Who would? Marnie Richards had blown his nomad world apart.

That only seemed to spur her on, and he reached between them. Rubbing her with his thumb, enjoying every little grip of her hands on his body and little moan in his ear or against his mouth. She pulled him closer, kissing his neck as she reached release. Clinging to him, she enjoyed the aftershocks of her orgasm.

'Babe,' Ash breathed. 'You're killing me here.'

She realised she'd been clenching down on him, and she smiled devilishly at him, moving her hips again. He knew his goofy expression had turned back to lust. He moaned as he thrust harder, deeper. Kissing her all over, telling her how good she felt. She did feel good. She felt like the only woman on earth. It was quite a heady feeling and not one he'd been expecting to feel when he'd woken up that morning. Or any morning.

His movements grew jerky, his voice less coherent. He kissed her fiercely, his thrusts quicker as he came. His kisses didn't stop, they just tapered off as he came back down to earth. When he did look at her again, he marvelled at just how happy and satisfied she looked. She lifted her head, slowly kissing him. A different kiss this time, he felt. The jolt was still there, but something else was there with it. When she pulled away, he checked her expression for clues as to how she was feeling, but she turned to the side. Her mind was on the monitor. He couldn't blame her for doing that. She stiffened when she saw him watching her.

'Sorry.' The rueful smile on her face was another thing he wanted to store up in his brain and remember. 'Habit.'

'Don't apologise for being a mum. It's kind of cool to see you two together.' He didn't imagine his wife and child when he observed Marnie either. Was that a good sign, or a bad one? Another thing to wrack his brain over later. When he was alone again. 'Give me a second.'

Getting rid of the condom in the bathroom, he walked into the bedroom just as she sat up in bed. He hadn't put anything on, but he didn't show any signs of being shy around her. He didn't feel shy, it felt…normal. Their time together was short, he was going to live it to the full. Squeeze every last drop of juice out of the moments they shared.

He got back under the covers, pulling her to him so she was snuggled in the crook of his arm. Her head on his shoulder, he could smell her shampoo. And him. There he went again, feeling all alpha wolf. Given that he wasn't about to start peeing on the Christmas trees surrounding her property, he squashed the thought. Next Christmas he wouldn't be here. He'd probably be a distant memory to Marnie. Someone would snap her up when she least expected it. He wasn't daft. If things had been…

'Violet will be up soon, but if she wakes up, don't feel like you have to go.'

'Okay.' He couldn't see her expression. Was she hinting for him to go, or reassuring him that he didn't have to? Nah, she didn't play games like that. Neither of them did. She meant what she said. Her stomach grumbled, and he realised with the events of the day, she'd probably not even eaten. 'Do you fancy some food? I cook a mean omelette. We can have a break from all the Christmas food. I'm maxed out on marzipan this week anyway.'

He patted his non-existent belly and Marnie pushed him till he theatrically pretended to flail at the edge. She pretended to save him, and, somewhere in the tugging and the laughter, he'd flipped her on top of him and they were kissing again. And doing other things that they probably didn't have time for. Violet truly was a good baby. She didn't stir till they were laid happily in each other's arms again. It felt so domestic, he should have been running. He didn't move anywhere but closer to Marnie.

By the time they were downstairs later, Violet having a feed while Ash cooked for them both in her kitchen, Marnie realised that having a new neighbour might just have been the lift she'd needed to finally move on fully. She'd realised something else too, as he brought her a steaming hot cup of cocoa, with whipped cream and marshmallows. She couldn't give a stuff about Oliver any more. The man could go off and rot in her back story. She was onto her new life. Sure, it might not involve this picture, but she'd have this memory, right? Of something that was easy. And hot to boot. After the day's events, she was definitely feeling the festive spirit.

Thinking about Christmas, her mind

wandered to thoughts about Ash and his circumstances. He always just seemed to work or be around here. While she knew he'd once been married, he'd not mentioned any friends, or any family. Maybe he really was alone? Did that make him lonely?

She thought back to her time after Oliver but before Violet. That had been a lonely time. Even with all her friends and family around her. So maybe Ash needed just as much fun as she did? She was wanting to get out more too. It was great going out with the girls but talk often did drift to men. Which left her nothing to speak about. She wasn't going to tell him about this, either, mind you. Not when it was only a fling.

She'd always hated that word. Holiday romance sounded better. A Christmas holiday romance. Why not? She sipped at her cocoa, watching Ash as he moved around her space. He filled every space he was in. He made his presence known without even meaning to. It was a shame that he spent so much time alone. She had a feeling she wasn't the only one in need of fun.

'Do you fancy coming with me to an engagement ball? I mean, Sophie and Roman's engagement ball. You've probably been told everything about it already. They've probably already invited you, but—'

'They did, and I'd love to go with you, Marnie. I'm already looking forward to it.'

*Wow.* She *was* going to have a good Christmas. She didn't need Santa this year. Just the neighbour she couldn't stop thinking about. As he brought over a pasta dish that made her mouth water, she thanked her lucky stars.

Ash nudged her arm, and her eyes fell onto his effortlessly. She always seemed to lock on. He did the same thing.

'Eat up.' He winked seductively. 'You'll

need all your strength.' He licked a bit of sauce off his thumb. 'For all that dancing.'

'Yeah,' she agreed, tapping her fork against his. 'We have to dance. It's Christmas.'

## CHAPTER TWELVE

MARNIE HAD HAD a busy day. Ash had been working, so she'd decided to finish the house completely for Christmas. She'd changed her sheets, cleaned everything. Taken Violet out in her carrier for a bracing walk. The stuff she normally did, but that day she'd had an extra spring in her step.

She was happy—really happy. She felt sexy and seen, she was killing it at being a mother, and she was involved with her neighbour. In lots of delicious ways that made her skin blush pink even in the cold Cornish weather. She tried to plaster on a normal expression, dulling her smile to an acceptable level. Her cheeks were hurting anyway from doing it all day.

She'd received the odd text from Ash

when he was on a break. Telling her he was excited for the night ahead. To see her again. Asking what they were both up to. He was good with Violet too, not hands-on, but he always asked about her. She'd noticed the other night, when he'd cleaned up. He'd put all Violet's bottles in the steriliser. Folded her laundered pink baby blanket and left it on the side. It showed he thought something of her.

Oh, God, she was thinking again. There was no time for this. Her mother was coming through the front door. No time for wistful thinking that was neither part of the plan, or possible. It was a holiday romance. Holiday. Romance. She drummed the thought into her brain even as her heart tried to pump it out.

*Oh, hell, no. Suck it up, Marnie!*

'Hello!' her mother trilled the second she was through the door.

Marnie steeled herself for some subterfuge. Aka hiding the fact she was sleeping with her neighbour every chance she got. Or was planning to anyway. While she could. While the feelings creeping in were still manageable.

'Hi, Mum!'

'Don't worry, the cavalry's here,' she called from the hallway. 'I'm so glad you're going out again, love. Where's my granddaughter?'

'Up here,' Marnie called down the stairs. 'Bring up that glass of wine from the side, would you?'

Minutes later, Violet was in the arms of her cooing grandmother, and Marnie was sipping at the cold wine and looking at her reflection in the long mirror.

'You look beautiful, Marnie. That dress is perfect.' It was a good find. It was a normal dress, just a size bigger than she'd usually wear, but she'd altered it. It had ruched, sweeping material across the tummy area, giving her confidence with her post-partum tummy. She loved her body for what it had achieved, but she wanted to feel good tonight. Confident and not giving a moment to adjust her outfit or worry about this tiny fold or that. Her body was beautiful, and she felt like that now. She knew the confidence had come in part from Ash, but it was down to her too. She felt as if she was finally living the plan. With a sexy six-foot-odd midwife bonus.

This dress was perfect for that. In a liquid, molten gold silk material, it made her feel as if she could hold her head up. She'd stuck with her usual sleek bob, knowing with a thrill that Ash loved it. It would no doubt be messed up by his hands by the end of the night. The thought of that gave her a frisson of butterflies in her stomach. Tonight felt really special. Oh, she knew that at Christmas most things felt special, everything was heightened. Good and bad, but it was more than that. She was thrilled to be going out with Ash. Even if her mother was there to witness them together before they left, with all her feelings on her face. Like mother, like daughter. She shrugged.

When Ash arrived at her door, he agreed with her mother about her dress. He looked at her in a very different way though. One that made her whole body quiver under the material.

'Marnie, that dress is beautiful. You look amazing.'

She smiled. Normally she would have rebuffed the compliment from men but, from him, she didn't feel the need to.

'Thanks, you look handsome too.'

He was dressed in a smart black suit, the hazel of his eyes sharper against the dark blocks of colour. His tie matched her dress, she noticed. A matching gold that shimmered when he turned. They would look like a couple. She wondered whether he'd thought of that. As if he had put thought into the tie. He'd obviously taken note when she'd told him what colour dress she was wearing.

'Nice tie—is it new?' she added, and

was rewarded with a smirk. A woman couldn't analyse a smirk, so she decided to stop trying. They weren't about games; they spoke about what they thought. If not fully what they felt. What she felt.

'Thanks. I thought it would complement your outfit, but nothing could beat that.' Her mother was busy fussing over Violet when she saw his gaze check on them. He leaned closer. 'You really are trying to kill me.' He half chuckled. 'You look amazing. I can't wait for tonight to be over.'

'Aww.' She was enjoying this. Teasing him. Driving him wild. 'No dancing?'

He gave her a look that almost had her reaching for the zip of her dress prematurely.

'Plenty of dancing. Nice and close.' He practically whispered into her ear. 'Hot and sweaty too, I should think.' He pulled back just as her mother turned back to face them. He gave her a smug little smirk, a secretive little move that made her whole body react and held out his arm like a perfect gentleman who never made a woman blush with his wicked ways. When he looked back at her mother, the simpering smile she gave him told Marnie that her mother was already sold. This was getting messier the more time went on.

'Shall we?'

She tucked her arm into the crook of his. Messy, but thrilling.

'Let's go. I'm itching to get on that dance floor.' She gave him an innocent enough look for the benefit of her mother, but her sultry eyes were all for him. The squeeze she felt on her arm as he tucked her in closer to him was all the answer she needed.

The evening was chilly, but thankfully mild for December. Their breath still condensed in the air around them as they walked away from her cottage. It wasn't too cold though, even though the snow was sparkling with the ice contained within the white surface. With her silk shawl, she felt quite comfortable. Unless this was just down to the heat of the man she was walking with. Her arm was still in his, and he'd slid it down for her hand and held it in his the minute their houses were out of sight. It was romantic, walking up to the hall. Everything was lit up. Fairy lights hanging high in the branches of all the trees they approached. It was like a fairy walkway, and the closer they got to the party venue, the bigger and brighter the lights and Christmas decorations grew.

'It looks like your front lawn,' Ash quipped, and she poked her tongue out at him. He'd helped her drag the rest of her lawn decorations out when he'd seen her struggling one day. It was yet another Christmas memory of him that had woven into her memory. When she was dragging them out solo next year, she already knew she'd be thinking of him.

The thought of it was enough to make her miss him. Even while she was by his side right now. She pushed the thought out of her head and watched it freeze in the snow. Tonight was not for thinking ahead. It was Christmas Eve. She was going to enjoy herself as much as she could.

'You should see some of the other houses around here,' she countered, thinking of one friend in particular. One who loved penguins and decorating even more than she did. 'Some of them make mine look like the Grinch's place.'

'I don't doubt it.' Ash nodded. 'Are you excited for tomorrow?'

'Very.' She beamed at Ash. 'Violet's first Christmas.' They could see the engagement party venue now, their feet picking across the grass. Ash was holding her tight, as though he was scared her heels would spike the ground and pitch them both forward. 'Oh, doesn't it look festive?'

Ash took a beat longer than normal

to respond. Actually, he had been a bit quiet since they'd left the house. Maybe he wasn't looking forward to tomorrow as much as she was? He'd already told her he'd put himself on the rota at Carey House for the day, explaining he'd happily take the hit, being the new guy at work, and a temporary one at that.

'Ash, are you okay?'

His gaze fell to hers, and his face changed again. He looked almost peaceful. The frown gone from his features as if it were never there in the first place.

'I'm great,' he said, nodding to the revellers. 'It looks like the whole village is here.'

'Oh, they are.' She had no doubt that most of the villagers would be here. Everyone loved Sophie and Roman. They were really happy as a couple. They didn't much take their eyes off each other. Even when they were talking to other people. Marnie could see them, looking for the other over shoulders and sides of heads.

It was cute to see. It made her heart ache a little too. They had their whole lives together. She had the rest of her maternity leave. If that. 'What do you think?'

She'd asked him an innocent enough question, but he couldn't tell her what he was thinking. The enormity of it was still hitting him. Leaving his cottage tonight and making the short walk to Marnie's house, he'd had a feeling brewing inside him. He'd felt it at work too, the more he recognised people who came to see him, saw babies come back in for development checks. Babies he'd delivered were out there now in Carey Cove. Some of them might even be Violet's classmates down the line. He had felt the odd pang of not seeing them grow up around him. How Violet would grow up without him. Hell, she wouldn't even remember him, not that he would expect her to. It would be better if she didn't remember a man who came and made her mother happy, then disappeared.

Would Marnie miss him? How long would it be until some other man saw what she was and set his sights on making Marnie his? Ugh. He'd been down this way of thinking before. Another man in her house? The thought made him feel sick to the pit of his stomach. He felt at home on their little street, in Marnie's house. He felt at home everywhere in Carey Cove. It was an odd feeling, but he was fast growing to like it.

He watched his colleagues around him. Nya and Theo were dancing, smiles on both their faces, as they watched Sophie and Roman pass by. He was twirling her on the dance floor, her laughing her head off. Her ring twinkled like a bauble under the festive tinted lights above them. He needed to shake this melancholy off. He wanted Marnie to have fun tonight—she deserved it. He wanted to make the night amazing. Just for her.

'Do you fancy a drink?' he asked her. He could do with one too. To take the edge off. Push the dark thoughts away from the corners of the dance floor.

'In a minute.' She grinned back. 'I'm enjoying the people-watching.' She pointed out one of the darker corner tables. Ash looked across, scanning till he saw Lucas. He didn't have Harry tonight, and he was obviously enjoying his night off. Kiara was giving him little kisses, the pair of them whispering to each other. Wrapped up in their own little world.

'Those two are so cute,' she breathed. 'I love the two of them together.'

He raised a brow, and she brushed him off. 'Hey, just because we've sworn off love, doesn't mean I can't appreciate romance.'

He looked back at Kiara and Lucas. He'd thought he was sworn off love too, once upon a time. He hoped Marnie didn't really think that. He already knew that they were lying to themselves about this just being a passing attraction between them. They both knew it was more than that. They felt it. He was sure of that.

This place, he was sure of that too. He didn't want to leave. He could really see himself living here, putting down roots again. It was such a surprise to him, but it was there, just the same. He'd felt so lost when his family had been taken from him. He'd given up the home he'd shared with Chloe. His parents had sold their farm, his childhood home, and moved away years ago. They wanted to enjoy as much of their retirement together as they could. It was always their plan, and he was thrilled for them. They were enjoying their life, happy together in their twilight years. Chloe's own parents had recently sold up their own neighbouring farm, starting a new chapter of their lives too. It seemed that everyone was moving on, while he just observed and moved from place to place.

Marnie had drifted away with a kiss on

his cheek, done on the sly. They weren't exactly hiding their status, but they didn't even know how to classify it themselves. A festive fling sounded tacky, and far off the mark from what he felt. He watched her chatting with her friends. She came alive around her friends. Animated hand movements, head thrown back in laughter. Marnie might have sworn off love, but it hadn't left her.

She had it in abundance for her daughter. He saw how loved and cherished Violet was. Marnie as a mother was a joy to see. She found it easy, and every little task was an honour to her. Not a chore. Even when she was tired, and half asleep, she still showed how lovely she was. How kind, how thoughtful. A man would have to be a lunatic to walk away from a woman like that. God knew, he would never have walked willingly away from Chloe. Oliver was a man he hated despite having never met him. Any man who would allow a bride like Marnie to escape was a fool, in his book. If he were Oliver, he would have married Marnie and never looked back. That would have been the best way to spend his twilight years. Being loved by a woman like that.

Marnie's eyes searched for his across the room, and she found he was already watching her. He could see her cheek flame, and as she looked at him with that knowing grin he felt his body stir. His heart too. He wanted this, but it was too messy. Too hard. Hell, he'd arrived late to this job. Perhaps he should never have come at all. The agency would have hired someone else. Marnie would never have known him. He would never have met someone he knew was a game-changer. He wasn't even playing the game, was he? He hadn't planned to. He hadn't planned anything. What was the point in planning when everything was lost? When he'd been on that floor, being fussed over by his sisters, that was all he would say to them.

*Wash your hair, Ash. You look like a scruff.*

*What's the point? She isn't here to see my hair. Run her fingers through it.*

He remembered how final things had felt. How ended his life had felt. Yet he was still here, expected to keep living it anyway. All he'd had left was his job, and a house he hadn't wanted to live in any more.

Marnie was still deep in chat with a small crowd, no doubt asking the work gossip and catching up on what she'd missed. When he'd arrived in Carey Cove, late and still a little broken, he'd felt as if he'd simply closed yet another chapter. He hadn' realised Carey Cove would make him yearn to open up another one.

The time he'd spent here at Carey Cove, developing relationships at work, spending time with Marnie and Violet, hanging out at their houses, it was all so happy. Hopeful. He'd felt a sense of belonging, and he felt it even more strongly now as he watched the people around him at the ball. He was sitting alone, Marnie occasionally looking over and meeting his eye with a sly smirk. A smile she only gave to him, he noticed. He felt territorial about that smile. It was just his. If he weren't here, would it disappear from her face for ever?

He winked at her and enjoyed seeing her flush before she turned her attention back to what Sophie was saying to the group of excited friends at the bar. Marnie was next to be served. He didn't have long before she was back. He thought of Chloe and Sam then, and recalled the last time he'd visited their graves. He'd sat on the grass by their headstones for the longest time, telling them that he loved them. That wherever they were, they were always with him. He wondered, now, what they would think if they knew about Marnie. How he'd met a woman who made him happy. A place that made him want to stay, instead of run. He was healing. He had healed a lot. Especially in this place, with these people.

Marnie was being served at the bar now, and he watched her smile at the barman. Her gaze flicked over to his, and he smiled over at her. Her whole face lit up when she smiled back, and it made his heart swell. He didn't want to leave this place. Marnie really was an amazing woman, and he couldn't imagine not staying put to see where this could go. It wasn't just the newness of it all, the twinkly lights and festive spirit overpowering his nomadic brain. When Marnie got back from the bar, he fully intended to ask her to be his girlfriend, to date properly. He'd tell her about his past, about Chloe and Sam, about the love and the loss he'd experienced, about how it had set him off on the path that had eventually led him to Marnie, and Violet, and a fresh start for them all.

He could find another job when it was

time for Marnie to go back to work, and he'd keep living next door. He could picture it, them spending their nights together, sweaty and laughing wrapped in bed. Walking on the beach, making sandcastles with Violet as she grew up in front of their eyes. He wanted that, he wanted all of it. He wanted Marnie. He couldn't wait to ask her to be his. To see this through. Together.

His phone buzzed in his pocket, and when he saw the name on the screen his heart lurched in shock. It was Chloe's mum calling him. The timing couldn't have been worse. He felt a wave of emotions. Guilt at what he was just thinking seconds earlier, how happy he'd felt before the call had interrupted his daydream. He was about to change his life, but it would change Chloe's parents' lives too. He was thinking about moving on, starting again, but although they'd physically moved, he knew that they would never be able to move on in the same way.

He loved them dearly, but their relationship caused him sadness sometimes. Like now. When he felt as if he was finally ready to move on, but he didn't know how to do it without causing more pain to others. He answered the call, trying to sound jovial and hoping she wouldn't hear the background music of the ball. He didn't want her to think he was out having fun all the time. Another pang of ridiculous, crippling guilt. He listened hard, but he couldn't make out his mother-in-law's voice above the noise. He headed away from where they were sitting, taking the nearest exit into the cold December air.

The ball was in full swing. Sophie and Roman were enjoying every minute of their engagement party. It was a beautiful event, all twinkling lights, tasteful Christmas decorations and Cornish ones too, making the party look magical. Everyone was dressed in their finery, and Marnie had had so many compliments on her dress, how glowing she looked. Little did they know the reason why. Her stomach still flipped at the thought of her and Ash together. The shocks he brought to her skin every time he touched her.

She walked over to the table she'd left him sitting at, champagne glass in each hand. She was going to ask him to stay over, she'd decided. Sure, her mother would raise her eyebrows and she'd be straight on the phone tomorrow to find out the gossip before she went to Christmas dinner. It would be worth it though. She didn't like the thought of him waking up in his house next door, alone. What was the point, when he could wake up next to her and have Christmas with them? She could easily share her first Christmas morning with Violet with him, then he could go in to work at Carey House as he'd planned, but be back to spend the evening with her.

The table was empty. Strange. She'd just seen him there. The napkin he'd been fiddling with was sitting on the table, right where he'd been sitting. He'd looked fine the last time she'd set eyes on him. She hadn't seen anyone speaking with him. She stood there, glasses in hand, scoping the room for his hazel eyes. The back of his head. No matter how she looked for him in the crowd, she knew he wasn't there. Had he left? Maybe it had all been a bit too much. Did he regret them? He didn't seem to show any signs of regret. He'd nuzzled her neck before she'd left his side to go to the bar.

She remembered where she was. Staring at an empty chair with two glasses in her hands. She took a seat on the chair he'd just vacated. Putting the drinks on the table without spilling them was no mean feat either. Humiliation was running through her whole body, making her hands shake. He could just be in the toilet, she reasoned. He'd pop back up any minute, and then she'd feel like an idiot.

She calmed herself down, checking

around to see if anyone had clocked her mini meltdown. If they did, they showed no signs of knowing. The party was in full swing, people in love all around her, having fun. She reached for her glass, drinking till the glass was empty. Having fun. As they should be. It was Christmas Eve, what had—?

Her phone was ringing in her bag. Grabbing for the clasp and dumping her glass on the table, she reached for her mobile phone. It was Ash.

She went to say hello but was stopped by a large crackle on the line. She listened. The line was awful. It sounded like the daleks were invading. She could hear a voice, faint. *Ash!*

'I know I need to go.'

What was he talking about? She listened again. The line kept dipping in and out of sound, the crackles cutting everything off. She had to force herself to keep the phone to her ear. As she did, she could hear Ash again. Mostly it was just his gravelly voice she heard, the words not quite making sense to her ear. Till three did that made her blood cool.

'Wife and son,' was what he said. It was clear to her ear, even as her mind took a while longer to process the news. So, he was married? And they had a child? He did regret their night together. Because he'd crossed the line. What the hell was he doing with her here, on Christmas Eve, if he had a wife and child at home somewhere?

She never went out, and she'd thought that he was worth it. For this short while. She'd even hoped he'd stick around after, not that she'd discussed it with him. Now all of that, all of this, was laughable. The line went dead, and she pushed the phone back into her bag. He didn't ring back. She had a feeling that she wasn't meant to hear his words. She wished she hadn't either.

She wanted to run home, tell her mother everything, get drunk and cry in bed. The old Marnie would have done just that. She was a mother now though, and she had heard only a snippet of a conversation. She owed Ash the chance to explain. She wanted to hear it, actually. She felt as if she needed to look him in the eye, if only for one last time. She was done hiding from men, and she couldn't write Ash off yet. She drank his glass, pulled herself together and headed back to her friends. Whenever anyone asked her where her date was, she smiled and told them that he had a personal situation.

Did he? she thought to herself. That was the million-dollar question.

She cared too much about the answer. He wouldn't be there tonight, in her bed, talking about their evening together. Or in the morning, when Violet woke up to discover that Santa had been. Not that she really knew, being that young, but Marnie didn't care.

*She still knew.*

She could do it alone. That was the plan

anyway. She pushed aside all thoughts of Ash, and partied with her friends, trying to dance and laugh her cares away. It was Christmas after all.

She had the best night ever, or she would have had. If not for Ash. Him not being there just felt wrong, even though she was used to seeing the faces that she'd spent her nights with pre-Violet. It felt weird Ash not being there. She came home alone, which also felt weird. Ash's house was in darkness when she headed to her own front door. She resisted the urge to sob. Pulling it together once again to greet her mother, regale her with enough happy stories of the night to send her on her happy way home with thanks from her daughter. She went to kiss Violet goodnight, smiling as she watched her snuffle softly.

'Happy Christmas, Vi,' Marnie said, before pulling the nursery door half to. The night light lit up enough of the room to make it cosy.

The little LED Christmas tree on her dresser was twinkling. Marnie looked at it for a long time, before heading back downstairs. She had a few more gifts to wrap, and a bit more wine to drink. Not too much. She wanted her daughter to have the perfect day tomorrow. But tonight, tonight she allowed herself to be just a little sad. And eat the rest of the mince pies, she realised as she headed to bed a couple of hours later. She needed to get some sleep or Santa wouldn't come, she told herself.

*What little lies we tell our children.*

That was her last thought before she fell to sleep, mince-pie crumbs still round her mouth.

## CHAPTER THIRTEEN

*Christmas morning*

VIOLET STARTED STIRRING in her cot around half-six, but Marnie had been awake watching the world through her open curtains. She'd watched the inky black night, and the stupid twinkling stars, and she'd got into a mood with herself. About being so bothered by another man who was a feckless idiot. A temporary relationship to boot. What was all that about? Was his child unborn? Was that the reason for the time limit, other than his leaving when the job ended? Obviously, there were other midwife jobs available in Cornwall.

Oh, for the love of safe deliveries, now she was mad at him for leaving, when she knew that was the deal anyway. She'd *wanted* that deal, she couldn't rewrite history now she was mad at him. She *was* mad at him, but she had known the score. She wasn't some lovesick teen, still hopeful of finding the perfect 'one'. She'd lived life a bit more to realise that was for the movies.

Violet's cry stopped her ridiculous hop-skip-and-jump thinking, and she decided to do what she did when she was at work. Switch off the personal-life button in her brain, and focus on the fact that Santa had been, and her baby was having her first Christmas. The best present for Marnie was undoubtedly spending the day as Violet's mum. She couldn't wait to watch her daughter, year after year, growing up and becoming her own person.

She leaned over the cot, her elated expression matched by her daughter's. It was the same all the time—they were just smitten with each other. Their eyes lit up at the sight of each other. Just like the mums and babies she'd seen over the years, when they all took their first look at each other.

'Good morning, my little gift. Happy Christmas.'

Marnie gummily grinned up at her. Her baby was growing up fast and meeting all of her milestones and Marnie was getting better at listening to the midwife training in her brain as well as the mushy goo that was her mum brain. Her mushy, sexy, messy brain goo. She'd lost a man, had a baby, met a man she could never have, been crushed by the man she couldn't have, and what else? Oh, yeah, she'd still wished for him. That moment, in the split second before she'd had her first coherent thought, her hand had reached across the bed. Not for Oliver, like some remnant of their relationship, but Ash. A man she'd spent far less time with. It was enough to distract a girl, but she was determined to have the best day.

Later on, the doorbell rang. That was the

moment that Marnie should have steeled herself. A pre-baby Marnie would have, but doting mum Marnie was so happy to see her daughter enjoying her first Christmas and enjoying babbling away to the music she had on low. They were both sitting in her rocking easy chair, her favourite place in the house when she was wanting to feel normal. Grounded. That was why she didn't think it would be Ash at her door, on Christmas morning. She didn't prepare herself, she just got up and went to the door, Violet in her arms.

She opened the door. It was Ash. Standing there looking gorgeous amongst the Christmas decorations in her front garden. Her heart beat faster even as her hand tightened on the door. She might have been thinking about him, but she didn't want to see him right now. She was so angry, and she didn't want her first Christmas with Vi ruined either.

She was all set to give him a tongue-lashing and boot him off her front step when she clocked his clothes. He looked dishevelled, crumpled up like a paper ball and half-heartedly smoothed back out. He didn't look as though he'd seen a wink of sleep. She hated that they were at odds then. She wanted to know what was wrong, even if it was to do with her discovery. They'd slept together once, and he was leaving. Perhaps they could just forget this had ever happened, fly under the scandal radar till he left Carey House? She could see the pain in his eyes, and she remembered all those other times the pain had been there. Giving her a clue to an answer that she felt sure she still didn't have. Was Ash really as devious as Oliver?

She didn't think so, and she wasn't stupid. Or easy to sway. Ash was the only man she'd been interested in since Oliver. But she'd already consigned him to history. He was still going to leave.

'Listen, I—'

'I'm really sorry for leaving you last

night, but it was important. I need to talk to you, Marn. Please, can I come in?'

His facc was determined, and she felt her feet step to the side to admit him. Here they were, back in the hallway, a very different mood in the room.

'Happy Christmas, Violet. Is that smile for me?'

Marnie looked at Violet, and she was. She was smiling. Right at Ash, her angelic face lit up as if he were Santa himself. Marnie's heart clenched.

*He's not ours, Vi. We can't keep him, baby girl. He's not ours to keep. He never was.*

'She smiled at you again!' She tried to pass off her feelings with a laugh, but it sounded dull even to her own ears. She got mad instead. The feelings had to come out somewhere.

'She only does it for me usually. You're privileged, clearly!'

'Sorry,' he mumbled. 'Not a great start. You seem angry.'

'I'm not angry,' she lied through her clenched, smiling teeth.

'I just came to say—'

'Happy Christmas?' she blurted out. She couldn't listen to his explanations about his family. She couldn't bear it. She just wanted him to go. In fact, no. She didn't want that. She found herself wishing she'd never set eyes on Ash Ellerington. She wouldn't be feeling like this now.

*Why does this hurt more than Oliver? How is this man so linked to my happiness?*

'Listen, I really can't do this today. I'm sorry. It's Violet's first Christmas and I—'

'I know.' He went to stand closer to her, but she backed away. 'Marnie, the last thing I want is to ruin your day. Hell, I never wanted to ruin any day, any hour of yours. I just need you to listen.'

'Ash, I—'

'Marnie, please. Hear me out.' He stood before her, his hands up in surrender now.

As if she were the one holding a weapon that would wound him. She couldn't hurt him now, not even if she tried. No matter what lies he had told, it was too late. Ash already had her heart. He'd wound himself around her heart tighter than Oliver ever had. She wasn't sure that she could get over this. 'I don't want to spoil your Christmas. That's the opposite of what I want for you.'

She wanted to slam the door in his face. She wanted to shut the curtains and hide away till his job ended and he left Cornwall in his rear-view mirror. She wanted that, right?

'Okay,' she half whispered. 'I'll listen.'

Ash's shoulders dropped half a foot with relief. She resisted the urge to tuck herself into the nook of his arm, pull him into her arms as she'd done before. How she was going to get through the rest of Christmas without his touch, she didn't know. The rest of her life? Impossible.

'Thank you. I'm sorry I disappeared. Last night. I didn't intend to do that.'

'Kidnapped by elves, were you?' Marnie's snarky tongue had woken up. 'You live next door. You have my number.'

'I know.' He ran his hand through his hair, sticking tufts up at odd angles. 'Marnie, I never meant to hurt you. I told you that, and I meant it. I got a call, last night. When you went to the bar. I never would have left otherwise, but it was important. It was Chloe's parents.'

'Chloe?' Marnie didn't want the answer to come from his lips, but she couldn't stop herself from asking anyway.

'My wife.' She flinched. 'Don't look at me like that, Marn. I can't take it.' She tried to move her gaze from his, but she just couldn't do it. 'I'm not married any more, you know that. I didn't lie when I said I used to be married.'

'Okay,' she plumped for. 'But you obviously didn't tell me the truth either. Not everything, and that's the same as a lie.'

She walked through to the lounge, taking a seat on the couch with Violet in her arms. He'd paused in the doorway, looking at the domestic scene before him. He pressed on, striding across the room and sitting next to her on the sofa without being asked.

'I was married, but that's not the full story. The truth is that Chloe, my wife, she died. I'm a widower, Marnie. I have been for a few years. Chloe died giving birth to our son. Sam didn't make it either. There were complications. It happens.' He shrugged bleakly, as if going over a memory. 'I went over and over the case. I was there in the room. It was just, too much.'

'I'm so sorry,' Marnie murmured. She held Violet that bit tighter. She'd seen him deliver babies, be around them. Around her daughter. She'd never had an inkling that his pain was from the loss of his wife and child. She could relate to that more than most. Longing for a child. The difference was, Marnie's was safe in her arms. Ash's baby had never had a chance at life.

'I thought you were in pain, but I thought it was just from the divorce. That you didn't want to get involved because of that. I understood that.' She brushed some water from her cheek. She was crying. 'When I heard you say about your wife and child on the phone, even though the line was terrible, I thought…'

'You thought I was a cheat, and no good. Like your ex. I would never hurt you intentionally, Marnie. That's not me. Oliver was a fool. I owe you an explanation. Will you hear me out?' Ash looked so devastated that Marnie could never refuse to hear what he had to say. Silently she nodded.

'Chloe and I truly were childhood sweethearts. We married quite young, and we were each other's world. When we discovered that we were pregnant we were so excited. Our families were too. Our parents were neighbours, and we were all so close. I loved Chloe, and my son. And after they died I truly believed that I was better off alone. I guess I stopped living too.'

He paused then, and Marnie gave him the space to continue with his story.

'But I did keep living, Marnie. Only I had to find a new way to live, a way without Chloe and Sam and the life we could have had and away from the memories that were suffocating me at times. And so I opted to move around the country, only taking short-term contracts. And those moves eventually led me here. To you, and to Violet. And honestly, for the first time in years, what I've found here, with you, and with Carey House, feels like it could be home.'

He swallowed.

'And last night, seeing you at that party, looking so relaxed and happy, and knowing what we'd already shared, I wanted to tell you everything. About Chloe and

Sam, but also about how I hoped that you might be starting to feel the way about me that I feel about you.'

He paused again, before taking a deep breath and continuing.

'Only before I could talk to you, I got a phone call. It was from Chloe's mum. It totally threw me. I realised how selfish I was being, I hadn't even given them a second thought. Hadn't considered how me falling for you would impact on them. I am the only other link left they have to their daughter; how would they feel knowing that I might be moving on with my life? The last thing I want to do is hurt them.'

'You love them,' she said simply. 'That doesn't change just because their daughter died.'

Ash nodded.

'Exactly. I can't break their hearts to gain my own happiness. I needed them to be okay with it. I don't want to live out of a bag any more. I don't want to be the new guy no one remembers. Not now. I want you to remember the hell out of me, but I don't want to leave you either. Ever.' He took the pair of them in, smiling. 'I'm not trying to get some ready-made family. When we met, I just felt such a jolt. I've never stopped feeling that. It's you and me now, and Violet. If you'll have me.'

'Ash, I—'

He locked the eyes she loved so much onto hers and strode over to her.

'Please, Marnie. Forgive me for not telling you the whole truth. I swear on everything I am, I will never hide a thing from you again.' He was in front of her now, and she looked up at his face, believing the words coming out of the mouth of the man before her. Everything clicked into place now. Why he was alone and not dating. The pain she'd seen in his features from time to time. They'd met each other in this Cornish corner of the world and healed each other without even realising it.

'I believe you,' she said, reaching up and touching his cheek. 'I trust you.'

His face lit up, and he bent to kiss her. Violet was taking in the whole scene around her from her vantage point of her mother's arms. Marnie thought she saw her grinning at Ash. The little madam knew the score from the minute she met him, Marnie thought to herself with a swell of pride. Her daughter was going to be a little genius.

'You do?'

She kissed him again, her pulling him in this time.

'Yes, Ash, I trust you. I'm so sorry you went through that.' She bit her lip, but the plan was screwed anyway. If it was in paper form, it would be crunched up firmly in the bottom of the wastepaper basket. 'I love you. I do.'

'Despite your best efforts?' he quipped, his arm around both the Richards women now as if he didn't want to let go. 'I love you too, Marnie. You blew my world apart.'

He got down on one knee in front of the sofa and pulled a small box from his pocket.

'Which is why I want to marry you. For us to be together, now. No games, no plans. Just us.' He took her hands into his. 'Will you be my partner in the next adventure, Marnie? I only want to travel by your side from now on. Make a home here in Carey Cove. Help raise Violet. Love you for ever.'

Marnie cocked her head to the side. This man. He was so off the plan he was the antithesis of it. Perfect for a lover. No strings. No drama, just the fun stuff. And yet there was more, the spine-tingling feeling when you were close to a lover, one who seemed to understand you as well as you did yourself. Even after a bumpy start when they'd clashed. She'd wanted to hog-tie him and chuck him into the salty cove when she'd first met him.

All the way through, the jolts of electricity between them had been undeniable. She felt them now.

'Ash, I would love to marry you. Where the hell did you come from?' She laughed, and he took a beautiful ring out of the box. He laughed with her, bending to kiss her.

'Hell, Marnie.' He kissed her. 'I came straight from hell, angel. Right to you.'

'Don't joke.' Her tone was cautious. 'Are you sure you want this? Is it not too soon? Do you need a—?'

He kissed her again, harder and more fervently this time, and she got the point. 'I'm not kidding, Marn. I came from hell. I hid all around the country, and then I came here. I was happy to blend into the background, helping other people start their families, see their joy and just move on. Save the mothers who got into trouble. It drove me, I guess. Till coming here. Till that day in the waiting room. When we touched, I just felt it. Even before then.

Your hair, your eyes. They made me look right at you. That was it. That was the moment. I just realised it. I didn't realise it at the time, but I came here for you.'

'I felt it too, but I resisted the whole thing straight away. I put it down to hormones, being tired. I don't know. It scared me, I guess. I've realised now though that my past was getting in the way. I had Violet on my own, but that didn't mean I had to stay alone for ever.'

'I get it,' he comforted her. 'After I was widowed, I just thought that I'd had my chance. I wasn't looking. Are you sure you're ready to trust someone like that again, Marn? I trust you completely, but if we do this…' He seemed to struggle for the right words, and she saved a breath. 'If we do this, we're all in. I know it's fast, but I know it's right.'

'I trust you completely.' She beamed at him. 'That's my point. I felt safe the minute we met; it was like…'

'Instinct.' They said it together.

'I just didn't trust the feeling as that, is all. I want to marry you, Ash. I think we'd be so happy.'

It was his turn to beam then. He moved closer, taking her hand in his. 'I want this more than anything, Marnie Richards.' He dipped his head to a smiling Violet. She already had him wound around her little finger. Like a daddy's girl. Marnie wasn't even shocked at the thought. It felt right. 'I love you.' He said it to them both, but his hazel eyes were looking into hers, and they sparkled when she said it back. Wow, she was becoming such a sap. She filled up with tears, and they kissed again.

'I love you too,' she told him again the second their lips parted. 'I'm glad you came here. Came home to me. Happy Christmas, Ash.'

'Happy Christmas, darling. The first of many.'

'That's the plan,' Marnie agreed, and they kissed over the top of Violet's head.

That night, they would do a lot of kissing, and a lot more besides. She wouldn't need the thermal reindeer pyjamas she'd bought herself as a Christmas treat, that was for sure. She reached under the tree and produced a present she'd bought for him earlier. A new sweater that would bring out the hazel in the eyes she adored.

'First Christmas as a family.' She smiled. Ash's kiss told her how thrilled he was with the idea. She felt the same way. The lightning bolt told her all she needed to know. She was going to live this adventure with Ash, and Violet, and enjoy every minute of their lives together. They had both been on very long journeys to find each other. It was time to enjoy it.

'Oh, no!' Marnie suddenly pulled away, her hand up to her mouth in horror. 'We can't do this.'

'Why? Yes, we can!' Ash was on his feet, startled, and Marnie giggled when she saw his reaction.

'Not us.' She reached out to him and

he pulled her up, steadying her and the child in her arms. 'I love you, but we have other plans.' She pulled a face. 'You have to work and we have to be at my parents' house, for Christmas dinner.'

Ash smiled as she added, 'Want to come after your shift? I figure you can help me tell them our news.' She pulled him in one last time to kiss him before they went and saw the world together. As they would stay, by each other's sides, for the rest of their lives.

# EPILOGUE

A LOT HAD happened in the last twelve months. Well, if Marnie looked back over the last few years, she wouldn't recognise her life now. She didn't have the wanderlust any more, even though Ash was keen to book a holiday soon. He wanted to start showing Violet the wider world, and she adored him for it. She could just see the three of them, jetting off to see the corners of the world.

She couldn't wait for her daughter to learn more, really experience life as she once had. Home was where the heart was though. She wouldn't trade any sunset beach in the world for this cold Christmas at Carey Cove. The world would still be there in January. The beaches and sunsets would wait for her family to discover them. For now, she had the magic of the season. Something the Cove had in spades. The girls had always thought so, but after the events recently in their own love lives, they were in no doubt of its existence. Any more than Marnie doubted the way she felt when Ash touched her.

The sparks still flew between them, a year on. She doubted she would ever get enough of Ash. She would often joke, call him her little 'plan derailer'. The anticipation of becoming Mrs Ellerington only brought her joy. Her fear of weddings and everything relating to love felt like a lifetime ago. Here she was, at their engagement party and she hadn't even brought any crucifixes or garlic around her neck. Ash had laughed when she told him.

*'Marnie,'* he'd murmured, pulling her close and making her forget what they were even talking about with kisses to her neck. 'You might as well face it. We are incurable romantics now. Thunderbolts and all.'

She'd agreed, with a little more persuading from the love of her life, and his kisses.

Last Christmas, Ash Ellerington had asked her to be his wife, and she'd agreed. They'd become a family that day, with Ash moving in pretty much the minute his lease was up. He'd barely slept there anyway. He always seemed to gravitate to her place, and soon she couldn't remember a time he wasn't there. She wasn't in a hurry to remind herself either.

They'd decorated the house together this year, Ash even getting a little competitive with Nya and Theo. Marnie thought it was going to be a duel at one point, Ash and Theo lining up on the beach, each armed with a Christmas novelty light-up penguin. It was hilarious, even Nya and Marnie had wound them up in the end. The kids thought it was amazing that their dads were so excited about trimming up. Ash had made good buddies with Theo. The two men were the perfect complement to each other, and they both adored their family time. Ash was working and living in Carey Cove, choosing not to work away and miss a minute of their lives together. He was there, full-time. A great father to Violet. The pair of them were like a comedy duo.

Ah, Violet. Her daughter wasn't quite a baby any more. She was her own little person now. She was still adored by everyone she met, of course, and she was a sociable little girl. Always babbling, waving and smiling at friends, family. She was a joy to have. Ash's face lit up whenever she was around, and the pair of them were inseparable. He'd crashed into Marnie's life, to cover for her while she became a mother, and then he'd shown her a world she hadn't thought possible.

The engagement party was perfect. Everyone had been so excited for the day to come, and now Marnie and Ash wanted to take in every little detail.

Together, they watched their friends

and family have fun as they took a moment to enjoy the Christmas Eve festivities. There weren't many Christmas babies happening for once, so they were enjoying the peace. Nya and Theo had walked in earlier and blown that apart though, with news of their engagement! The whole place went wild. The pair of them had said that marriage wasn't on the cards, but obviously love had changed their minds and Marnie and Ash couldn't be happier for them. Nya was a woman Marnie loved dearly, and she couldn't be happier for her. After everything they'd been through together, the fact that their happy endings were here was amazing. Marnie couldn't wait to watch her walk down the aisle to Theo, their family and friends all there to share in the pure joy of the day. What it meant for them, starting their new lives together after finding each other. She squeezed Ash's thigh, as if to remind herself that he was still there.

'Reminds me of our festive proposal,'

his deep voice rumbled against the shell of her ear, and she felt the familiar, still-take-your-breath-away jolt that she always felt from him. 'Another wedding, eh? You lot are all going to be married off, you romantic bunch.'

She laughed. After Sophie and Roman had got married, Lucas and Kiara weren't too long after. Now Nya had fallen too. No more single girls, Marnie mused. They all looked so happy. Hope, Theo and Nya's adorable foster daughter, so beautiful with those Cornish blue eyes. Her brown hair was held back with pretty clips, sparkling sequins depicting little penguins. Nya always did dress her well.

They often went shopping together on their days off, the kids ending up in soft play while the two of them talked shop. Marnie had never imagined getting to do that with her friend. It made the trips all the sweeter to have. Hope was a lovely little girl. Marnie hoped the two of them would be as close as their mothers when they grew up. Perhaps they would even train as midwives. The next generation running Carey Cove. Hope and Violet, delivering babies. It would be just too perfect.

Hope was laughing at something, Violet giggling right along with her. Those two loved to play. They were always giggling. Just like their mothers, she thought to herself. Nya caught her eye, and the pair of them laughed. They knew they were thinking the same thing. It warmed her heart.

'I love how close Hope and Violet are.' She reached for Ash's hand, and it enveloped hers as always. He brought it up to his mouth and kissed the back of her hand. She forgot her train of thought for a moment, but Ash picked up the conversation.

'Sophie's pregnant too,' he said softly. 'They're just waiting to tell Roman's parents before they announce it.'

'I know.' She smiled. 'I'm so happy

for them. I love how you care about our friends.'

'Of course I do.' He put his other hand over hers, sandwiching it between his mighty hands. 'It got me thinking too.' He nodded back to the two playing girls. 'It might be nice for Violet to have another kid to play with.'

She heard that. Loud and clear. 'Mr Ellerington, are you suggesting we have another baby?'

He pretended to consider it for a moment, and then waggled his brows devilishly. 'At least one.'

'At least one!' Marnie exclaimed. He shrugged.

'At least. I figure a boy might be nice.' He looked over at Violet, a grin of adoration crossing his features. Violet and Ash were two peas in a pod. She adored him. Had from the start, Marnie remembered. She gave her first proper smile to her new daddy. Even before Marnie knew, Violet did. She knew the man she'd met at Carey House was supposed to be in their lives.

Marnie followed his gaze, looking at her daughter, who was dancing comically with some of the other little ones. She was off now, making her own first little steps into the world. Ash followed her like a papa bear when they were out in Carey Cove. A big, tall protective warrior dad, his two fingers always wrapped in a pudgy little hand as Violet clung to various surfaces. She was always babbling away to him. Ash hung off every little word and declared her a genius daily. 'What do you think?' He took her chin between his fingers, kissing her. 'For once I can't tell what you're thinking.'

She snorted. 'You could never tell what I was thinking!'

Ash looked shocked. 'In what way?'

'In every way I wanted to do things to you.' She smiled cheekily at him. 'We didn't play games, but we both hid a little something. That afternoon, after we'd first made love, I looked at the three of us in the kitchen, and I just knew that I would find it near impossible to let you go.'

He was looking at her in wonder, the same way he'd locked those hazel eyes onto hers when she first told him that she loved him.

'You never told me that,' he half whispered. 'I felt exactly the same. You know that, right?'

She kissed him to say yes, she did. When she pulled back, another daydream popped back into her head. She'd had it the other night. They'd taken Violet to her mother's and gone for a meal with their friends. A real Carey House couples' night that had been such a good time. When they'd gone home that night, the house had been quiet without Violet, and as she'd drifted off, hours after they'd gone to bed together, she'd thought of something. How nice it would be to have a sibling for Violet. For Ash to have a child of his own. Oh, they didn't do the labels. He wasn't a stepdad. He was a father to Violet—he'd been there from the start. It wasn't that, but she wanted more children. With Ash. She wanted to give him a child. They'd never talked about it before, but she had considered since last Christmas.

'You sure? The girls always said that I was a little bit of a tyrant when I was expecting Violet.' His belly laugh told her he didn't much care about that. Her heart swelled, as it did every day around him. With Ash coming to Carey Cove, it was as if her life had been completed. He was the missing piece. The thought of bringing another child into that, having a baby with her husband by her side. It was not part of the plan, that was for sure. She thought back to how steadfast she'd been on her actions. When she'd been expecting Violet, she'd decorated the nursery alone. It would be nice to do those things again, with Ash. She narrowed her eyes at him. 'Are you being serious?'

He looked at Violet, who was playing with Hope, Nya watching them both with a huge grin on her face. Looking back at his beautiful fiancée, he couldn't imagine anything better.

'I don't think we should put any pressure on it, but yeah.' He leaned in, kissing her slow. Just how he liked to kiss the second love of his life. The one he'd never looked for, but now he couldn't stop. God, whenever she was out of his arms, he looked for her. He was ridiculously in love. The way she felt in his arms, it still took his breath away. Waking up to her every morning was bliss. Her friends were now his friends too, and he was already seeing the babies he'd delivered grow around him when he was out and about. A couple of mothers were already seeing him for their next pregnancy. He could already imagine walking Violet to school, seeing those babies at the gates in their little uniforms. He wanted that, and more. He wasn't scared any more. He knew that even if lightning struck, the jolt of love between them would be enough to be worth every moment. 'Have you not thought about it?'

'I've thought about it.' She took a sip of her champagne. 'I wanted it to come from you, I think. If and when it was time.' She gave him a small little smile, her sexy bob making her look fierce but adorable.

'I know what you went through to get to Violet, and with Sam… I just knew that it wouldn't be straightforward for us.'

He talked about Sam, and Chloe now. Marnie had told him not to hide the precious photos he had. The life he had with Chloe before was part of him. Sam was related to Violet, through them. One day, they'd tell Violet about Sam, too, and his mother. How they were dearly loved but didn't get to stay on Earth. It was important to Marnie that Ash not forget them, and Ash loved her all the more for it. They'd even travelled to see their graves together. Marnie had even spoken to them both. Ash never knew what she had said. He'd taken Violet to see the flowers instead. He figured what they were talking about wasn't for him to hear. It was between them.

The more he'd thought about it lately, the more it made sense. He was ready to be a father again. Sam and Violet were perfect, and he knew that a baby would be the icing on the cake.

'I love you, Marnie. I've thought about it for a while. You already made me a daddy. I love being Violet's father, and I want to do it again. Soon, hopefully.' He grinned, giving away a little of his eagerness. 'I would love to have another child with you, Marnie. It would be just…'

His smile took over his speech, not letting him get his words out. Seeing Violet play with Hope in front of them really cemented what he'd been feeling lately. They'd been together a year now, but it felt so much longer. They loved life on their little lane. They had talked about moving somewhere a little bigger, to buy a house together. They'd never got very far. The truth was, her cottage was home for them. Their little lane was home. Besides, they had an extra bedroom to fill. Why bother leaving paradise?

'Perfect?' she finished for him. They grinned at each other. Ash pulled her closer, his heart swelling with the jolt of electricity she gave him with her touch.

'I think so.' He dropped a kiss onto the bridge of her nose. The one she scrunched up when she was concentrating, or laughing heartily at work, or with Violet. 'Well, let's practise, eh? See what happens. No pressure. PCOS didn't stop you before, and we have contacts in the right field.' He thumbed over to the other people who lived and worked in Carey House. It was true, the gang would be thrilled. They would be ecstatic for all three of them. 'Besides, we haven't spent any time in the hallway lately.' His hazel eyes grew darker, lustful. 'Be a good place to start.'

She shook her head at him, but she was grinning.

'You're naughty.'

'I know,' he retorted. 'You love it.' Another sneaky kiss attack from him. He always did that when they were close by, talking. She'd be doing the dishes one minute, kissed senseless the next.

Marnie guffawed with laughter.

'Oh, really?' She looked back at the girls, who were being twirled around the dance floor in the arms of Kiara and Nya. 'You really want a baby?'

'I really want a baby, Marnie.' He leaned in. 'Our baby. What do you say?'

One look into those hazel eyes, and she knew the answer. It had been hard to get Violet. Frustrating, expensive, maddening. Then she thought of what Ash had been through. Losing Sam before he got a chance to know him.

With the job that they did, they were better placed than most to know how things could go wrong. Not work even. Fail. Complications happened. Emergencies happened. Not every baby delivered got the privilege of drawing their first breath. They knew all of the lows, but, looking at the girls, she remembered the highs too. All the lives that had come into the world. Some of the babies they delivered would be in the same classes as Violet, and their baby. Marnie knew that even knowing everything that could go wrong, it didn't stop people. That was life. You rolled the dice, strived for happy. That was what they would do. Strive for happy, and if the worst happened, they had the other to lean on.

'Okay, deal.'

He waggled his eyebrows again, taking her answer in. 'Really?'

'Really. I love you, Ash. Let's make a baby.'

'Woman,' he said, sounding like a cowboy, 'I simply can't wait.' He took her hand in his, kissing the back of it like the Prince Charming he was. 'I love you.'

'I love you too,' she declared to him, as she always did when it threatened to burst from her lips anyway. For a cynical woman down on romance, she was much happier than the engaged woman who'd been on that beach in Bali. She wouldn't be back there for anything. Here, in Carey Cove, right where she had laid her roots, she felt freer and more hopeful than she ever had. There was a big, wide world out there, and she couldn't wait to explore more of it with Ash, and their children. Showing Violet the world with him by her side? With their other children? That sounded like a plan worth living for.

Mrs Marnie Ellerington-to-be could not wait to get started. Christmas at Carey Cove really was magical, she decided.

Looking around her at the family they had, the love and attention, the care and the shared experiences. It really was a special place, and this Christmas would be no different. It was all part of the plan.

* * * * *